HIGHLAND RETRIBUTION

3 THE BAND OF COUSINS

KEIRA MONTCLAIR

DEDICATION

To my daughter Christy,

Thanks for always being an inspiration. Hope this works!

THE GRANTS AND RAMSAYS IN 1280s

GRANTS

LAIRD ALEXANDER GRANT and wife, MADDIE
John (Jake) and wife, Aline
James (Jamie) and wife, Gracie
Kyla and husband, Finlay
Connor
Elizabeth
Maeve

BRENNA GRANT and husband, QUADE RAMSAY
Torrian (Quade's son from his first marriage) and wife,
Heather—Nellie (Heather's daughter from a previous
relationship) and son, Lachlan
Lily (Quade's daughter from his first marriage) and hus-
band, Kyle—twin daughters, Lise and Liliana
Bethia and husband, Donnan—son Drystan
Gregor
Jennet

ROBBIE GRANT and wife, CARALYN
Ashlyn (Caralyn's daughter from a previous relationship)
and husband, Magnus—daughter
Gracie (Caralyn's daughter from a previous relationship)
and husband, Jamie
Rodric (Roddy)
Padraig

BRODIE GRANT and wife, CELESTINA
Loki (adopted) and wife, Arabella—sons, Kenzie (adopted) and Lucas, daughter, Ami (adopted)
Braden
Catriona
Alison

JENNIE GRANT and husband, AEDAN CAMERON
Riley
Tara
Brin

RAMSAYS

QUADE RAMSAY and wife, BRENNA GRANT (see above)

LOGAN RAMSAY and wife, GWYNETH
Molly (adopted) and husband, Tormod
Maggie (adopted) and husband, Will
Sorcha and husband, Cailean
Gavin
Brigid

MICHEIL RAMSAY and wife, DIANA
David and wife, Anna
Daniel

AVELINA RAMSAY and DREW MENZIE
Elyse
Tad
Tomag
Maitland

CHAPTER ONE

1284, the Highlands of Scotland

CAIRSTINE MUIR HAD A SICK feeling deep in her belly. The feeling didn't stem from the fact that her wee son had run off again and they'd been unsuccessful at finding him, but from a troubling thought that had entered her mind.

A small part of her would be happier if they never found her son; if another clan took him in and offered him a better—and safer—home.

Steafan, or Steenie as she called him, had disappeared after he'd gone into the bushes to pish, or as he liked to say, "go pishy." At only five winters, the lad was one braw soul who was prone to distraction, often ending up in a completely different area from where he started. Cairstine constantly reminded him to focus, but he was just a wee lad. His father often gave him a thrashing to hammer in the lesson, but it rarely stuck with him.

Unfortunately for Steenie and for Cairstine, being the son of Greer Lamont was not easy. Greer and his brother Blair were cruel, sinful men. They'd killed her parents and the rest of her clan in front of her, and Greer had then taken her hostage and called her his wife. She'd never said a vow to accept him, nor would she have, even though her dear mother would rightfully have told her they lived in sin.

Greer didn't believe in marriage. In his mind, he owned Cairstine and that was all she needed to know. That arrangement suited her fine, because she never would have agreed to be his wife. Better that she was forced to live in sin. Nearly everything Greer did was sinful.

"Steenie!" she called out from atop her horse, wishing she'd never agreed to come out on this small journey. Greer had said they'd be patrolling the area, watching for something, though he'd not said what. She knew better than to ask, but Steenie had begged to ride along. He loved getting outside the castle and knew he couldn't go alone. On rare occasions, Greer gave in to him. This had been one of them. She could almost say she regretted it, but had she not come along with them, he'd have no one else to help him find the lad. He'd sent his guards off to search for the shipment of goods they expected, deciding at the last moment that the two of them would search for Steenie alone.

How she wished her wee son would get away forever. As much as it would break her heart, she'd prefer to see him free of the brute who controlled their lives with his fists. If Steenie ever managed to get away, she'd follow the first chance she got. She'd tried to run away once with the lad, but she'd learned her lesson. Greer had made sure she'd never do it again. But if she didn't have the lad to worry about, things would be different.

"Steenie, where are you?" Her gaze searched the area again, not seeing the beautiful Scottish landscape for what it was.

There had been a day when her gaze would take in the lush green forests, the rolling hills standing so majestic in the cool Scottish winds, but rarely did she notice the wonders of nature any more. How she used to love the sweet fragrance of heather mixed with pine, or the whistling of the wind through the towering oak trees, just waiting for the days their leaves would turn into the glorious golds and reds of autumn. They used to stir a deep sense of pride, but no longer.

She hadn't seen those sights in years. Instead she only saw desolation and despair wherever she looked. How could the landscape change so much?

It hadn't, she had.

There had been two days in her life that had forever left a lasting impression on her. The first was the day her parents and brother had been killed, and the second was the day she'd nearly died trying to escape Greer Lamont with her young son in tow.

Those two incidents drove everything she did, changing her life and her focus to only one thing—protecting and loving Steenie. She no longer cared about herself, if she lived or died, only her son. She would protect him until she took her last dying breath, no matter the size of the beast she'd have to fight.

A shadow crossed over her soul and she started, staring up at the clouds overhead, even though there were none. The feeling reminded her of those two days, sad but separate, long ago.

Both days she'd had a terrible foreboding in the morning, a premonition deep inside her, that some chance occurrence would change her life forever.

She was experiencing the same intuition, the same hunch deep in her core. In her past, the feelings had come over her as though a priest had covered her with a dark shroud, but this was slightly different.

This shroud was light, billowing in a warm breeze.

What could that mean?

Greer rode up beside her. "He's not here, but I see there's a celebration at a nearby clan, the Drummonds. I'm hungry. We'll head into the courtyard and see if Steenie snuck inside. As long as we're there, I'm eating. If we don't find him, we'll head back to our land."

Cairstine nodded her agreement because she'd learned it was best to always agree with him. Greer Lamont was a bastard. So much so that she'd given him that name with a bit of kick at the end.

Bastart!

How she hated him. She followed him toward the sounds of revelry inside the bailey of a large castle. The gates were open, so perhaps Steenie had found his way inside. This was a celebration for the villagers of the clan, the same type she'd seen put on by her own clan many moons ago. Some clans allowed outsiders in, some did not.

Greer wasn't interested in finding out, instead barreling inside as though he belonged. She followed him, her gaze seeking out someone small. If Steenie were inside, she hoped he'd hidden himself well. Or, better yet, that he'd told his story to one of the clan elders. She'd wished to tell him what to say about his sire should he ever have the opportunity, but he was too young to recall such things and too young to understand when it would be appropriate to reveal his story. She feared it would slip out to Greer and they'd both be punished for it.

Perhaps she should have prompted him, or perhaps someone would take pity on him. After she moved inside the gates, she hurried to keep up with Greer. As usual, he paid her no mind. He'd made sure a year ago that she'd never voluntarily leave him again. Stay or die was his simple motto.

If it weren't for Steenie, she'd choose death.

Once they were inside the courtyard, she scanned the area again for a young laddie, but there was no sign of her son. She almost lost sight of the *bastart* in the crowd. These men were tall and strong; her gaze fell on several handsome faces. It occurred to her that any of them could likely challenge her captor and win. But if Greer caused trouble, they might beat her, too. Just because her sire had not beat women did not mean others wouldn't readily partake in the unconscionable deed.

She continued to trail Greer, just now recognizing the hunger sounds in her belly. When had she eaten last? How she wished she could turn to any of the men and whisper, "Help me." But she'd learned long ago not to go against Greer or Blair Lamont, and she'd learned the hard way. She would never give the *bastart* the opportunity to use Steenie against her again.

The basic needs in her life mattered little. Survival and protection of her son were all that were important.

Greer found a table full of plump meat pies, pushing others aside to get toward the front. The only problem was there was another man who'd already reached the front of the table, and he was perusing the different pies as if searching for something in particular.

That forced Greer to wait, and he'd never possessed any patience. He was about to make a spectacle of himself. How she wished he would just be patient, but the Lamont brothers loved attention. They considered themselves more important than anyone else, so Greer would no doubt decide the man at the front of the line was in his way.

Never mind that they were in a strange place. Never mind that they'd not been invited. That would not slow Greer, even in this rare occasion that he was without his brother.

She examined her surroundings: a beautiful keep with intricate crenellations on the curtain wall, three towers as big as she'd ever seen, a large bailey filled with well-kept cottages, and multiple buildings for the skilled of the clan. It all spoke of a thriving, wealthy clan, as did the multitude of guards stationed on the curtain wall and the sheer number of guests enjoying the festivities.

This was Clan Drummond. When her mother had been alive, she'd mentioned the Drummonds, how wonderful the laird Diana and her husband Micheil were. She even recalled the expression on her mother's face when she'd explained to Cairstine that women could be lairds, and good ones, too. The Lamonts were not far from the Drummonds, less than half a day away, but this was the first time they'd been here since returning to Muir Castle four years ago. They didn't believe in being neighborly, so they kept to themselves. It was no surprise that Steenie had found his way here when they'd been out traveling away from home.

But her gaze, so trained to find the sweet young lad, didn't see him anywhere.

Mayhap she'd been looking at the situation completely wrong. Perhaps she'd wish that Greer would be true to his usual self, become belligerent, and this clan would beat him, putting him in his rightful place as a barbarian. Maybe she'd be so lucky that they'd show him what it felt like to be a prisoner.

Greer gave the man at the front of the line his shoulder. "Hurry up so I can grab my share."

The dark-haired man turned around and said, "I'll take my time, arse."

"Hellfire you won't. Get out of my way."

Cairstine almost gasped when she caught a full glimpse of the man challenging Greer. He was shorter than several of the strapping Highlanders at the gathering, but hell, his handsomeness surpassed them all. Dark hair, dark eyes, and the most muscular shoulders she'd seen in a long time caught her attention enough that she couldn't look away. Greer was undeniably a good-looking man, too, but his black heart made him ugly to her.

Greer grabbed the stranger's tunic by the neck and lifted him off his feet. The handsome lad counteracted with his fist, delivering a blow that launched a resounding crack, causing the *bastart* to let go of him, stand back, and grab his nose. He then grabbed Greer's leg and tossed him onto his back, giving him no time to respond. He leaned toward Greer, his boot on his chest, and said, "I said I'll take my time."

To Cairstine's surprise, Greer calmed down. "My apologies," he said. "Take what you want and move on." The look in Greer's gaze told Cairstine this wasn't over—he'd only conceded for the moment. So, he was wise enough not to start a fight with a courtyard full of strangers…she wouldn't have thought it.

When the man stood back, Cairstine reached for Greer to assist him, but the boor shoved her hands away. She whispered to him, "Greer, please. Can we not leave?" Clearly, Steenie was not here. It was best for them to move on and continue their search elsewhere.

She glanced up to find the handsome man staring at her, his gaze intense enough to make her blush.

How she wished she had the courage to speak.

Take me away. Save me, save my son, from this ogre.

That foreboding, that shroud, covered her again. This time she couldn't tell if it was light or dark.

Before she could think any more about it, Greer bounced to his feet, his gaze now locked on the other man. He whispered, "Don't touch me, Cairstine."

She stepped back and dropped her gaze to the ground. The gown she wore was a shabby garment of green wool. Why would the man stare at her so? It couldn't be her looks, as she'd lost any enticing qualities years ago. All light had gone out of her along with her hope for a new life. Greer often took pleasure in reminding her of how unsightly she'd become. If that's how he really felt, she wondered why he didn't just do her the favor of turning her out onto the street. Surely, her life would be better as a homeless wench than kept unwillingly in the bleak and tarnished walls of her clan's ruined castle.

As the handsome lad stood there, still staring at her, another man with hair as dark as night came up behind him. The two had a similar look except the new man towered over every other man in the courtyard. The newcomer asked in a loud enough voice for all to hear, "Need help, cousin?" A fair-haired man stepped up to join them, offering his support as well.

The handsome lad replied, "Nay, I've handled it." He grabbed a meat pie, and after a nudge to his cousin, the three of them stepped away.

As soon as they turned their backs, Greer spun around and slapped her hard across the cheek. "Do not ever embarrass me again. I am capable of standing on my own. I don't need your help." She'd learned not to cry out when he hit her—he'd hit her again if she did—but she couldn't stop the reflexive action of her hand going up to her cheek, as though rubbing it would take the sting away or stop the bruise that would appear the next day.

The brawny lad whirled around with the reverberating sound of Greer's slap, just in time to see her reaction.

The fury on his face shocked her. He closed in on Greer and demanded, "Did you just hit a lass? Someone who could never hurt you? Someone who is smaller than you and doesn't have the muscle strength you have? Surely a big man like you doesn't need to pick on a wee lass to make himself feel stronger, does he? I thought I'd already shown you just how weak you really are." He continued to step closer toward them, and Cairstine could see the fire in his gaze. She reflexively took two steps back.

Shite, but they were in trouble now.

Greer glanced back at her, a small grin on his face. "Cairstine? Did I hit you?" He had his hand on her wrist. His fingernail scraped her tender skin on the inside; a veiled warning that if she did him wrong, he'd slash deep, something he loved to do. Many of his abuses were done this way, hidden from the people who could help her.

Cairstine dropped her hand from her face and shook her head. "Nay. He didn't hit me. A bug bit me, and I slapped it away."

"Leave it be, Braden," one of the other lads said.

Braden. That was her protector's name. Why couldn't she

have a man such as Braden, one who didn't hit women in order to feel in-control?

Greer grabbed three meat pies and shoved two at her, then yanked her along behind him.

She glanced over her shoulder at Braden, wishing she had the nerve to mouth the word "help" to him, but she didn't. The only one who would suffer from that action would be her.

———◆———

BRADEN GRANT HAD A DIFFICULT time controlling his temper. He memorized the bastard's face and his plaid, though he didn't recognize it. He'd find him. He'd find him and set the woman free. She didn't have to ask for help for him to know that she needed it.

Braden yelled out, "Someone needs to teach you how to treat a lass, arsehole." The man kept walking, ignoring his taunt. He scowled at his cousin Connor, who'd called him off. "You should have let me at him."

Connor's gaze followed the man out through the gates. "This is a celebration for our cousin's wedding. There's no need to disrupt it, but I wager we'll see him again. I never forget a face."

David wasn't their cousin in truth, but he was related to the Ramsays, a clan so interwoven with the Grants, they were embraced as family.

Still, as happy as Braden was for David, all he could think about now was *her*. There had been something about the look in her eyes, the sadness and despair, that had called to him. She was a beautiful woman with golden hair plaited around soulful green eyes. Silky strands of her hair had escaped her plait, the gold surrounding her face in a halo effect against her strong cheekbones and pink lips that begged to be tasted. Women did not usually affect him so strongly, which made her presence even more alluring. He would have disrupted the festive gathering itself to save her. Of course, the obvious question was, would he just be doing more damage by meddling where he wasn't invited? He seemed to have a talent for finding mistreated women, wanting to stand up for them, but he'd been around enough to learn some lasses willingly stayed with cruel men.

The first time he'd seen a man slap his wife—rather, the first time he'd been old enough to do something about it—he'd swung his fist in an attempt to protect her. Only she'd attacked him in return, shouting that he had no right to hurt her husband.

His cousins had teased him ever since, the same group of cousins who surrounded him now. Connor and Roddy, his closest friends.

Daniel Drummond, David's brother, joined their circle noiselessly, catching him off guard.

Roddy grinned at him. "Since you're as talented as a ghost, who was that? Were you close enough to see him?"

Daniel grinned back, looking quite proud of himself. "Aye, I've seen him before. Lamont. Blair or Greer. They're brothers and they're both nasty."

"Greer. She called him Greer. You must be correct." Braden's gaze followed her through the courtyard. He noticed she was turning her head from side to side as if searching for something.

Or someone.

Daniel rolled his eyes at him, and Roddy said to Braden, "You doubted him?"

"What?" Hell, but the lass had distracted him. He'd missed part of their conversation.

Roddy pressed him. "Daniel. The one who knows everything and can travel anywhere undetected? You doubted him?"

He had to laugh. "Nay, Daniel. I'll never doubt you. You sure know how to avoid attention when you'd like, Ghost."

Braden watched the fool toss his wife up on a horse and then climb up on his own horse not far from hers.

He sensed something unsavory was afoot. This was not a normal couple, nor was the woman, Cairstine, with the man by choice. "Do you know where their castle is? I'm going to pay a visit to him on the morrow," Braden said.

"Nay," Daniel replied. "He used to live south of here, but they let their castle fall to ruin, so they left. Don't know where they went. I heard a tale that they occupied Muir Castle, but my sire has gone there on a few occasions only to find it empty, though I'm not sure how long ago his last visit was."

Roddy grinned, clasping Braden's shoulder. "I think we'll be hunting on the way home. Am I not correct, Braden?"

He whispered, "Not to worry. I'll find him."

Green. Her eyes were green like the newest buds in the spring. She'd glanced at him on the way out. But he'd also noticed something else.

Those green eyes were full of pain, and he vowed to fix that, whatever it took.

He left his cousins and went off in search of his uncle Micheil, who he guessed would have more information about the Lamonts and where to find them.

He found his uncle gathered around the hearth with two others, chatting.

Uncle Micheil said, "Braden, are you enjoying yourself? Getting enough to eat?"

He nodded, not wishing to be rude. "'Tis an impressive feast, Uncle Micheil. But there's one thing spoiling my appetite. If you don't mind, I have a question for you."

"What is it?" his uncle asked, giving him his full attention.

"Do you know the Lamont brothers, Greer or Blair?"

"Aye, stay away from them," Uncle Micheil said. "What's brought this up?"

"I just had a wee run-in with Greer, I believe."

"Here?" his uncle asked, standing tall and leaning toward him. He guessed from his posture that he was quite familiar with the Lamonts.

"Aye," Braden replied. "He didn't think I was moving quickly enough at the food table. I also didn't care for the way he treated the lass he had with him."

Uncle Micheil quirked an eyebrow at him. "The Lamont brothers ran their castle into ruin and then abandoned it a long time ago. I heard they'd found another castle not far from here, probably just a bit farther north from our land, but I've not seen them. Not like I've been looking of late. It's been several years since they disappeared. If they're surfacing again, it's a blight Scotland doesn't need. I'd hoped they'd left for Norse lands or even England."

"Well, according to Daniel, one of them was just here. He tried to shove me a few times, but I straightened him out."

"The old Greer Lamont would not have backed down unless he was alone, and even then, I'm not sure he'd be wise enough. Bullheaded without a doubt." Uncle Micheil gave him an odd look. "Be careful with him. You don't want to be caught alone with the two brothers. They can be brutal."

"He wasn't with his brother. He had a woman with him. He grabbed a few meat pies and left, dragging her behind him."

"And what are you asking me? If you've a mind to go after him, don't waste your time," Uncle Micheil said.

"Even though he mistreats women? I'm quite sure he slapped her face behind my back, and I'd like to teach him a lesson."

"Braden," Uncle Micheil said, "I applaud your honor, but I'll give you a warning. If you wish to teach him a lesson, wait until you can bring a large number of Grant warriors with you. The Lamonts love to fight. 'Tis all I remember about them. We were all glad to hear they'd moved north."

Braden nodded. "My thanks, Uncle. I guess we have some business to attend to when the festivities have ended."

Uncle Micheil clapped him on the back. "If you find aught unusual, call on your Band of Cousins. I wouldn't be surprised to find out the Lamonts are involved in something devious. They've never been the sort to believe in honest, hard work."

The Band of Cousins consisted of Braden, Connor, Roddy, and six others, all dedicated to stopping a terrible blight that had been uncovered by Micheil's niece Maggie and her husband, Will. They'd located a hidden network that sold women and children, mostly across the waters to foreign lands. Maggie had stopped an earl who'd tried to sell three bairns under the age of ten, and David's new bride narrowly escaped another group of traders. According to what they'd heard most recently, however, the network threaded throughout Scotland. It was, quite appropriately, known as the Channel of Dubh, the dark channel. His uncle Logan, Micheil's brother, also worked for the Scottish Crown and was doing all he could to stop this atrocity from continuing.

"Aye, we'll contact Will and Maggie if we discover aught. But I wouldn't be surprised if 'tis true. I could tell the man had no honor at all."

What he didn't say was that he had to find Greer Lamont, or he'd be haunted by the pain in that lass's gaze for the rest of his life. He'd wait for his cousins or his clan's warriors to launch a full-scale attack, but what could it hurt to wander on his own this eve while the others drank their ale? Following their trail before the weather erased it could be paramount to him achieving his goal, one he wasn't about to let go.

Whatever it took, he'd find her and do his best to keep her safe.

CHAPTER TWO

—————◆—————

CAIRSTINE FEARED THE ABSOLUTE WORST. Had Steenie been caught by a boar or a wolf? They'd traveled for two hours in different directions, trying to cover any possible path the lad could have taken on foot, but they'd found no evidence of her son. They trekked by moonlight on a well-trodden path back to their castle, and they were nearly there. Steenie had never wandered that far before. Their original ride had only been to the edge of their land, yet they'd searched beyond that and not found any evidence of the lad.

Her stomach rumbled and she wished she could stop it. She'd eaten one of the meat pies, one of the best she'd ever had, but Greer had gobbled up the other four, taking one of hers. She'd learned a long time ago to eat when something was put in her hand, or else he would finish it and leave her with nothing.

Her horse was tiring. She'd fallen a distance behind Greer so that he was far outside her line of sight, and she feared they wouldn't be able to catch up to him. With wolves and other wild animals around, she didn't wish to ride alone.

A child's screams echoed to her from afar, so she encouraged her horse to gather the last reserves of its energy and race toward the sound, praying it was Steenie.

Greer's horse stood munching on grass, so he had to be afoot. After scanning the area, she finally noticed him off to the right, crouched over something. She dismounted and ran toward him.

"Did you find him?"

"Aye, I found him," Greer yelled, after the sound of three loud thwacks carried to her, followed by her son's pained wails. "And I'm beating his arse for taking off."

Cairstine closed her eyes, unable to watch her son's thrashing. How she wished he were still a babe in her arms, the only place he'd ever been safe. Tears misted her eyes as she listened to Steenie taking his punishment.

"But Papa, I was looking for food for us," he cried out. "Here, I brought you some hazelnuts."

She opened her eyes in time to see Greer take the proffered treat and throw it on the ground before he tossed the lad back over his knee to thrash him a few more times.

The sound of a wolf finally stayed Greer's hand. He stopped to listen for the proximity of the animal, then tossed Steenie toward her.

"Close your mouth. Stopping crying like a wee bairn and act like a man."

"He's not a man, he's a verra young lad, Greer." She held her arms out to Steenie as he flew into them, hugging her around the waist so he could bury his face in her brat to hide his tears.

"Get on your horse." He gave curt instructions that she was expected to follow without question. Her thoughts were never asked for or appreciated. "That wolf isn't far. We need to get home." He raced ahead of her to his horse, not attempting to assist her at all, and before she could blink he'd already taken off. He never even glanced back to make sure that she had mounted or gotten safely on her way.

Bastart! How could he leave the two of them out here alone with a wolf not far away?

She picked Steenie up, though he was getting too heavy for her, and hurried back to her horse. Glancing over her shoulder, she was assailed by the vision of a wolf closing in on her with its razor-sharp jaws open and ready. She shook her head to rid the image from her mind. There were no wolves in front of her, just her imagination playing with her fears again. She made haste and lifted her son up onto the horse and then led the animal to a nearby rock so she could mount behind him since the *bastart* was already long gone.

Steenie hugged her middle as soon as they took off, angling his body so his backside didn't bear the brunt of the galloping horse.

"Steenie, are you hurt anywhere else? Where did you go?" She tugged him in close while he sobbed, doing her best to keep on the path behind Greer.

"I...I wandered away because after I pished in the bushes I saw a rabbit. I wanted to kill it with my sword to make Da proud of me, but it got away and I couldn't find either of you. Why did it take so long for you to find me?" His wails continued, though she guessed his bottom was quite sore at the moment. Greer often thrashed Steenie, but he refused to discuss it with her, saying she coddled the lad.

She remembered his exact words. "I'll make him into a man, just like my sire did with Blair and me. One day, you'll thank me that he didn't turn into a helpless creature like his mother. For now, you need to stop protecting him. You have no say over my actions, and I'll do as I wish with the lad." That was the only order he'd ever given her that she refused to follow, simply because it was impossible for her *not* to protect him.

She ran her hand through his long golden locks, massaging his scalp the way he liked. "You must have gone too far when you looked for a place to pish. We couldn't find you. Next time don't stray so far away."

He hitched and hitched. She pushed his hair back from his face, wishing she could peer into his green eyes. She was so grateful Steenie looked more like her than Greer, but she couldn't help but wonder if that was one of the reasons the man was so brutal to his own flesh and blood.

"Take some deep breaths or you'll fall off the horse, lad. Did you get hurt at all?"

"Nay," he took a deep breath and sighed. "Why must Papa thrash me so? I just want to make him proud of me. Sometimes I don't like him."

Cairstine didn't even attempt an answer. The relationship between a sire and a son should be special. She knew that from watching her brother and her sire. For some odd reason, no matter how many thrashings he received, her son still adored his sire and would do anything the man asked of him.

It was something she didn't understand. How she wished it were different.

"Papa is trying to teach you to be more thoughtful of your actions. 'Tis all. Don't take the thrashings to mean he doesn't love you." She did her best to stay far enough away from the *bastart* so he wouldn't overhear their conversation. Although he was no longer in her line of sight, she'd learned to always have an eye out for Greer Lamont. He was often unpredictable.

"He doesn't love me. He never says so, and *you* always tell me you love me." He peeked up at her, swiping the tears from his face and his runny nose.

"Aye, he loves you. 'Tis different for men. They don't oft speak of love."

"When I have a lad of my own, I'll love him so and I won't ever thrash him."

She couldn't help but smile at the thought of her son of five winters all grown up with a lad of his own.

But a different thought surfaced in her mind. Greer was not part of that happy picture she envisioned for her and Steenie. How she hoped to be far away from the Lamonts by then, long before their brutality would be able to cloud Steenie's sunny vision for his future.

For a long time, she'd dreamed of a Highland warrior coming for her, fighting Greer and his brother, and reclaiming the castle in the name of her clan. Her mother had told her stories of powerful warriors, even English knights who jousted in tournaments, who would go to battle over a woman, either to protect her or to ask for her hand in marriage. Her mother had claimed a wonderful, honorable man would come to ask her sire for her hand one day. But those were just childish fairytales to her now and did her no good to hold onto.

For the first year after the attack, she was certain someone would come and save her, realize that she'd been kidnapped and kept against her will. But that someone had never come, probably because the Lamonts had been wise enough to keep moving through caves and abandoned huts for nearly two years before returning to recapture Muir Castle. They'd had enough of an army to take it back from the reivers they'd found inside.

Her childhood home had been reduced to ruins after the battle and whatever had been done by the reivers. The keep still stood because her sire had built such a strong castle, but the beautifully crafted furniture and the fine touches her mother had added had mostly been destroyed. Even the few fields her sire had built up to be used for crops had been destroyed. Little remained to remind her of her parents and their beloved home.

Once they felt it safe, the Lamonts had moved into Muir Castle, claiming it as their own. They'd built their army of guards up and were planning some new venture, though Cairstine had little knowledge of what the venture was other than that it promised lots of coin.

Unfortunately, if anyone had inquired, the Lamonts lied about how they'd come to live here and been left alone, or so she'd been told. Their claims were apparently unchallenged, even by their king. Her hope of being rescued had diminished with every passing moon.

Even though her parents had led her to believe differently, life wasn't always a happy story.

At least she still had Steenie. She kissed the top of his head after he fell asleep against her soft bosom, his favorite place. She plunged ahead, hoping Greer would be too exhausted when they arrived at home to take notice of them. She'd sneak Steenie into her chamber and the two of them could snuggle together in the cool night.

The sound of a horse behind her stilled her. Thankful that Steenie was asleep, she glanced over her shoulder, fear prickling the back of her neck as she twisted her head around.

The horse slowed, then stopped when a man came abreast of her.

It was the lad from the festival. She didn't speak, just pulled Steenie closer to her.

"Greetings to you," he said as his gaze scanned the area, probably searching for Greer.

She nodded, afraid to speak for fear of what she would say.

Take me away.

"My name is Braden Grant. I'm not here to hurt you."

Hell, but the man was gorgeous. Even in the moonlight she detected a chiseled jaw covered with a bit of stubble and soulful eyes that called to her. There was something about his countenance, his demeanor, that was different. He had the air of a powerful man, but not threatening or nasty like the Lamonts.

Take me away. Please.

Instead of speaking her thoughts, she said, "What do you want?"

He cleared his throat and swallowed before he spoke. "I wished to make sure you were hale. I know he hit you. The bastard shouldn't hit someone smaller than him." The fury in his gaze caught her. He was a man of honor, he had to be. Even though she saw anger in his gaze, she knew he would never hurt her.

Steenie's head popped up from inside her arm. "Papa hits me, too. Why? I tried my best."

To her surprise, the fury in his gaze increased for a few seconds before it disappeared. "How old are you, lad?"

"I'm five winters."

Braden's gaze moved to the lad before landing back on hers. "He's your son?"

She nodded, surprised to see what she thought was disappointment in his expression.

"If you ever need assistance, I'd be glad to help. I'm from Clan Grant, north of here."

A thought crossed her mind unlike any she'd ever had before. Why didn't she go with him? Beg him to take her to some clan where she and Steenie could live? She could work as a kitchen maid, a house maid, anything to get her away from Greer Lamont. Her head drifted toward the direction that Greer had gone. If it hadn't been for the punishment she suffered the last time she tried to get away, and Greer's evil threats…

But her savior could be standing right in front of her. He could protect her from Greer.

The *bastart* suddenly appeared out of nowhere. "Cairstine, get your arse home. Did you forget my promise?"

Without another thought, she mumbled a brief, "Thank you for your offer, my lord, but we must go."

She'd never, ever forget Greer's promise to her. The very thought of it often gave her nightmares. Flicking the reins of her horse, she closed the gap between herself and Greer, not daring to glance over her shoulder until Greer had turned around. But by then, the Grant warrior had already left.

Why hadn't he stolen her away? Done the same that Greer had done to her? Kidnapped her. Used her. Controlled everything she did. She knew the answer without a doubt.

Braden Grant was an honorable man. But he'd followed her. Why? Just to see if she were hale? She forced the man from her thoughts, back to the circumstances of her true life. He was gone, and her life would never change until someone killed Greer Lamont.

Perhaps it would be her.

When they made it back home, she steered the horse to the stables and Corc, the stable master, came over to help them down. Greer was already long gone.

"Lad, you look as though you've been crying again," Corc said.

How Cairstine adored the good-hearted man, who'd served her family for many years. He was the only one left from her clan who still worked with the Lamonts. They'd needed a stable master to manage their horses and coerced him into staying by threatening Cairstine's life. If he ever went away from the Lamonts, they'd simply kill her. Corc had agreed, to her relief. Unsurprisingly, he was also the only male who acted as a good role model for her son, something Steenie desperately needed.

"Aye, Corc. Papa thrashed me again for getting lost." He allowed Corc to lift him off the mount, then he tread gingerly around the grass to see how much pain he was in. Cairstine had seen him do the same many times.

She could swear there was a misting in Corc's eyes as he shook his head. "Foolish lad." Corc's hair had turned gray soon after the Lamonts took over. He had a crooked smile and an easy laugh that touched her heart.

Steenie stopped in front of him and stared up. "I'm not foolish, Corc. I was trying to kill a rabbit for Papa. When I got lost, I could not find anyone." His hands rubbed his bottom.

Corc leaned over to whisper in Cairstine's ear. "I meant to say your husband was foolish, not your son."

She leaned back to whisper her response. "You know full well he's not my husband, Corc. Never said the word 'aye.'"

His pained look told her he didn't like Greer any more than she did. But he also cared to protect her reputation. He merely patted her shoulder as he leaned down to console her son. "Och, lad. You must be aware of your surroundings at all times in the Highlands. We have great big wolves out there, or do you not believe us? I've warned you before."

"I'm not afraid of a wolf." He stared at the ground, his self-worth totally crushed by the *bastart*.

"Mayhap not, but you should be afraid of your da. Have you not learned that yet? I always stayed away from my da's swinging hand. And when I got older, he started swinging belts and even a paddle."

Steenie's eyes widened at the thought of being hit with something stronger. "How big was the paddle?"

Corc held his hands out, greatly exaggerating the size of the paddle. His hands only stopped fanning out when he looked up and saw Cairstine's look of doubt, her hands on her hips.

Steenie never noticed his mother, instead staring at Corc's hands. "I don't want Papa to hit me with a paddle that big." He dragged his gaze from Corc to his mother. "Does Papa have one that big?"

"I'm not sure, Steenie." She ruffled his long locks.

"He might," replied Corc. "So you best be on your good behavior."

"But men are not supposed to hit someone smaller than they are. That man said so." He lifted his chin with such determination that Cairstine would have smiled if not for the content of his message.

Corc shifted his gaze to Cairstine and then back to Steenie. "Maybe that's true. Where did you hear that?"

How she hoped Steenie would never make such a statement to Greer.

"The man wearing a red and green plaid and riding a horse. He told Mama that. I heard him. He said Papa hit

Mama."

"Shush, Steenie," Cairstine darted next to him to cover his mouth with her hand. "Do not let Papa hear you speak of that man. He'll not be happy and thrash us both."

Steenie stared up at her, properly frightened so he nodded, then took off toward the keep, forgetting his pain until his rapid movement reminded him of it. He stopped, only to limp slowly away.

"Sorry, lassie. Just trying to help him. He needs to be afraid of Greer. Who is the man in the red and green plaid? You know whose plaid that is, aye?"

She lowered her voice to barely a whisper. "He said he was a Grant. Do you know them?"

Corc quirked his brow. "Know them? Surely you've heard of the Grants. They're the most powerful clan in the Highlands, allies to the other strong clan, the Ramsays. How did you come upon him here? We're a good half a day from the Grants."

"Aye, I've heard of them, but I don't think much on it. He was at the Drummond festival. Had a run-in with Greer over meat pies. He followed me to see if I was hale." Her hand rubbed her cheek again. What did it matter? If someone was to rescue her, it would have happened long ago. It had been six long years. She'd lost all hope.

"Greer hit you and a Grant warrior witnessed it?"

"Aye, but you're wrong that the man witnessed it. He heard the crack and came to my defense. But I lied and said I slapped a bug away."

"Greer had his hand on you as a warning. I know his ways." Corc patted her shoulder. "I don't like to get your hopes up, lass, but that could have been the best thing that ever happened to you. I knew the old Grant stable master, Mac. They're a fine clan, and they do not take kindly to men beating women."

"I almost wished I'd gone with him on the spot," she said, brushing the tear away from the corner of her eye. Why hadn't she? Because the name Grant had meant nothing to her. Now she knew better. Greer kept her isolated from everything.

"Was he alone?"

"Aye. But at Drummond Castle, there were two others with the same plaid who banded around him against Greer."

"Lassie, I'm going to give you some advice, e'en if you did not ask for it. Do not run from Greer unless you have half of the Grant warriors there to protect you. I heard the threat Greer made against you, and I believe he meant it. Tread carefully. But if you do have the support of Alex Grant calling you ahead with a band of his warriors, promise me you'll go and never look back."

"But Steenie…" She swiped at another tear.

"I know, lassie, I know you love him. Take him with you if you have the opportunity. But do not be foolish and risk your lives for freedom. Someday, the Lord will make things right. Believe that your sire is watching over you, too. He'll find a way, but he won't do it until he's sure."

"I know, Corc. You're like a sire to me now. If only young Steenie had a da half as much a man as you…" She sighed and followed her son.

Every day she walked into the keep she forced herself to remember the good days. Six years ago, the Lamont brothers had taken the Muirs by surprise in the middle of the night, bringing over a hundred men with them. They'd committed murder over and over again. Since her sire was chieftain of the Muirs, the Lamonts had searched for him first.

She and her brother had come out to the balcony and then run down the stairs, following the villains out of the doors. They'd frozen at the top of the stairs of the keep, incapacitated by the sight before them. The Lamonts had dragged her parents into the middle of the courtyard, then proceeded to kill them both. Greer, the heartless devil, had killed her mother without flinching, and Blair had taken his knife across her sire's throat. Her brother had gone tearing down the staircase, bellowing, before she could move to stop him. She was just fifteen at the time, and he was two years older. Even if she had tried to hold him back, he would have broken out of her grasp, hellbent on revenge. The second that Greer spotted her poor, beloved brother, filled with rage and anguish, he thrust his sword straight into his belly. Her brother had been unarmed and stood no chance against the fools.

Her brother had died with her parents, along with all the staff except Corc. Everything she'd known had disappeared in a wash of blood.

She'd wished she'd died with them. How things had changed in their absence, and all her joy faded along with them. Steenie was the single spot of brightness in her awful existence. The only comfort she had now was that she was certain her family was in heaven.

Unfortunately, for her own foreseeable future, she would remain in hell.

CHAPTER THREE

———◆———

BRADEN AND HIS COUSINS ARRIVED back on Grant land a fortnight later. They'd met briefly with Will and Maggie, then traveled to Will's grandfather's home to work on the cottage they were building as a meeting spot for the Band of Cousins. The three-room house was nearly done when they left. The meeting room would hold a large table for ten, along with a hearth and shelves for cooking. The other two chambers were for sleeping, one for lads and the other for lasses, with several pallets built into the walls.

They'd left behind their Ramsay cousins to build the table and chairs, and Maggie and Will would make heather mattresses for the pallets.

The couple had followed up on the last known location of the Channel of Dubh, but they'd found no useful information, so they were headed back to Edinburgh. The problem was that the whole illegal enterprise was swathed in shadows—the men in the network did not all know one another or who was in charge.

Meanwhile, Braden couldn't concentrate long enough to stop thinking about the lass with Greer Lamont. He should have followed her to the castle, wherever it was, but he'd been alone and known that would have been unwise. Connor and Roddy had convinced him it was best to go back to Clan Grant and see what they knew of the Lamonts before searching out his castle.

He'd been surprised to see Cairstine had a son, but he shouldn't have been. She was clearly Lamont's wife, so even though the way Lamont had treated her had struck every nerve in his body, it wasn't a reason to steal her away, no matter how she stirred his loins.

He'd done his best to forget her, but he failed miserably. The pain in her gaze haunted him.

Braden and Roddy settled at the Grant dais for the midday meal when they returned. Their sires, Brodie and Robbie, joined them, and Connor came in a while later with his sire, Alex.

They spent most of the meal talking about David Drummond's wedding and the events around it, which only made Braden more anxious. When the conversation came to a natural pause, he asked, "Uncles, do either of you know aught about the Lamont brothers?"

Uncle Alex asked, "Lamont? Nay, should we?"

Braden said, "I met Greer Lamont at the Drummonds on the night of the wedding feast, and 'twas not pleasant."

Uncle Alex quirked his brow but waited for more information.

Roddy chuckled. "I'd say 'twas most entertaining. Do you not agree, Connor?" He gave their cousin a teasing look, making it all too clear that he intended to taunt Braden and hoped Connor would join in on the fun.

Connor picked up on it deftly and added, "Entertaining and memorable."

"How was it memorable, son?" Brodie asked. "Was your temper involved?"

Hellfire, but hadn't they drawn out of his father exactly the response they'd wanted? How they loved to taunt Braden about his temper. Aye, his temper was stronger than either of theirs, but he'd learned to control it, hadn't he? When would they stop assailing him? "Papa, I *did* control my temper."

His cousins laughed and clapped each other on the backs. "Did you now?" his sire asked, his two uncles taking everything in.

"Aye, I could have pulled my knife, but I restrained myself. The brute shoved me first, and any Grant would retaliate over an intentional push. Am I not correct, Uncles?" He glanced at the two men, who continued to observe the scene without interfering, Uncle Robbie with a smirk, and Uncle Alex with a stonier face that kept his thoughts a secret.

He continued, "I thought I handled myself well enough."

Connor snorted.

Braden glared at Connor. They'd seen the same thing, hadn't they? Lamont was a mealy faced swine. "I was at the table trying to choose a meat pie when the fool shouldered me hard from behind, telling me to hurry up. I didn't feel I needed to hurry at all. We were at a reception for the wedding, not a jousting tournament. I don't even understand why he was there. He's not an ally of Uncle Micheil's."

Connor said, "The gates were open. Anyone in the area was welcome after the wedding. The couple had gone on their way, so the food and festival were for all."

Uncle Robbie asked, "And how did you let the man know that you didn't wish to hurry, Braden?"

"After he pushed me and grabbed my tunic, I retaliated by punching him in the face."

"Sounded like you broke his nose," Connor said. "And then you flipped him onto his back and set your boot on his chest, but nay, you did not hold him at knifepoint, so I suppose you're right."

Braden shot Connor a look that indicated he would be next to receive his fist if he didn't stop his jesting. "So, no one knows of the brothers?" he asked, hoping to steer the conversation back to his original goal and that someone would give him a clue leading to the woman named Cairstine. "The Drummonds told me they used to live in the

Lowlands but deserted their castle because 'twas in ruins and made their way north five or six years ago, though they're uncertain where. I was told they are a bad sort, the type who would attack unprovoked."

Uncle Alex said, "Sounds to me like they're not worth chasing, so best if you let it go."

"Only one problem with that," Connor said.

Uncle Alex stared at him, waiting for his youngest son to finish his statement as he leaned back in his chair.

Connor cleared his throat and explained, "Lamont had a woman with him, and Braden thought he slapped her. I must say she was quite a beauty. In fact, he followed her to see where they went, and even spoke to her, but she and her wee lad followed Lamont northwest of the Drummonds."

Uncle Alex sat up straighter in his chair, a familiar fury in his gaze. His wife had been mistreated before they met, and he was always moved by the plight of women in distress. "If 'tis true, then we need to find her. I'll send a group south of here, search the area for any signs of new dwellings. Last I heard, the king hadn't made any decisions about the Buchan Castle. Mayhap they've joined others there."

Uncle Robbie's gaze narrowed. "Hmmm. I've just remembered something. Alex, do you recall what happened to the Muirs a bit southwest of here?"

Uncle Alex said, "The Muirs are closer than you think, probably a half day's journey. I wish we'd been home when that tragedy took place. Whoever ransacked that clan did their damage and left. They were never found or identified."

Uncle Robbie said, "That in itself was odd. Muir Castle was a fine building. It doesn't make sense that the attackers would have left such a fine keep behind. Why not take it over?"

"Because our king would never have condoned such a massacre. The guilty group went into hiding, for certes. No one ever knew who committed the evil deed, or why. The Muirs were a peaceful people." Uncle Alex stroked his jaw in thought.

"Did we not send guards there when we returned?" Brodie asked.

"Aye," said Alex, tipping his head back to prod his memory. "Our guards buried the Muirs and some of his men at the request of our king. They identified the laird, his wife, and his son. Never found the daughter. She must have run away."

"Or a servant managed to get her out and sent her off to a relative somewhere."

"Possibly," Alex murmured, still deep in thought.

"How old was the daughter?" Braden asked, a sick feeling roiling in his gut. "Do you recall her name? I think I heard her called Cairstine."

Uncle Alex thought for a moment and said, "The son was nearly a man. The daughter was a year or two younger, but I don't recall names. I remember the Muir talking about how his wife could no longer have bairns after the daughter. Both were hale and looked close in age when I visited him last. That must have been seven or eight years ago. I'd guess she would have been ten and three or four, the son near ten and five or six summers."

"What coloring?" Braden asked, fearing he already knew the answer.

"Both were golden-haired. Why?" His uncle had to suspect what he would suggest next. He gave Braden his full attention, his gaze narrowed.

Fury burned a path through Braden. "What if the villains who attacked the castle killed the rest but kept the girl?"

"Why?" Uncle Robbie asked. "Was the lass you met golden-haired, Braden?"

"Aye, she was. Difficult to guess her age, but she had a son around four or five summers."

Roddy answered without hesitation. "If you'd seen her,

Papa, you wouldn't ask why Braden cannot get her out of his mind. And she didn't look overly pleased with her situation to me."

Connor nodded in agreement.

"But this would have been five or six years ago," Uncle Robbie added.

Uncle Alex rubbed his chin in thought. "This doesn't make sense from what we know. Anyone who would kill that many would do so with the intent of taking over the castle. Muir had built a fine fortress. Where did the murderers go? How had they never been seen by anyone? My men asked many residing in the huts between here and Muir land, but the only answer they received was that the killers seemed to be ruthless and random in their intent. After the blood bath they left behind, the bastards moved on quickly to prevent their detection. All the neighbors were aware of the massacre and hid in caves, many said."

Braden sighed. "That part doesn't fit, does it?"

"Nay, but that doesn't mean there's naught to it," Uncle Alex said. "When I send a patrol out, I'll instruct them to travel to Muir Castle. I assumed 'twas deserted. Our men had been there again two years after the massacre and only found reivers. I reported this to our king and told him it was nearly uninhabitable because of the damage done by the marauders. I was actually thinking of acquiring it, but 'tis in a valley that is often flooded during the rains. The great hall has even flooded on occasion. Crops don't grow well in what little boggy soil they had, and the Muirs were forced to find fields elsewhere because they lost so much of their harvest too late after realizing. No one who knows the area would want it."

"Why are you interested, then, Alex?" Uncle Robbie asked.

"To keep reivers out of it. I should have done it long ago. I thought we could attempt to improve the land, build it up. 'Twould take much work, but we need to work to keep Scotland strong. And if we occupy the castle, mayhap we may find clues as to who committed the atrocious act.

"For now, our focus should be finding the lass and the Lamonts. Hopefully, we'll find out more about Muir Castle if we travel to that area. We have plenty of warriors to do both. If it weren't for King Alexander and his grieving of late, he'd probably have awarded the land to someone long ago. Though some have called it worthless, I'd now like to determine that myself."

Braden had a difficult time containing his excitement. "I'd like to go along, if you don't mind, Uncle Alex."

"Jamie and Jake are off on a different mission. Braden, I'll put you in charge of the patrol, but don't act rashly. Roddy and Connor will go with you, and you may choose your men."

Shocked to be given the duty, he did his best to hide his pleasure at being trusted enough to lead. "I promise to make you proud, Uncle." With that settled, Braden got up from the table and nodded to his family. "I'm going to visit Ronan's family. I have some other business to attend to."

"Braden, why not wait until the morrow?" his sire asked. "'Twill not be a pleasant visit."

"I know, Papa. 'Tis why I'd like to get it over with. I'll be heading to the Muirs on the morrow." He stepped away and headed out of the great hall.

This was something he had best do alone. His uncles and his sire would have certainly checked on the family while he was gone.

Braden's close friend Ronan had taken his own life several moons ago. According to the tales he'd heard, the man had lost all hope after seeing Marta, the woman he had loved and planned to marry, with another. Mired in darkness, he'd ridden his horse to the steepest cliff in their area, dismounted, and thrown himself over the edge, leaving the horse munching grass. Braden, Roddy, and another friend had climbed all the way down to bring his body back up for his family. He'd hit so many rocks during the fall that he was nearly battered beyond recognition. They'd done the best they could, straightening bones out, fixing torn skin, but it had still been a ghastly sight.

Braden's trip to work with his cousins had given him the chance to focus on something other than his friend's death, which had been a profound relief.

Now he was back, and he would pay his respects again to his friend's family, even though he'd already done so multiple times. The truth was that every time he stood on Grant land, he missed his dear friend. He couldn't imagine how Ronan's brothers and mother felt every day.

His steps slowed as he approached the family cottage in the outer bailey. Ronan's father had added to the original hut, making it one of the nicer cottages on the grounds. He knocked on the door, a small part of him wishing no one would answer, but the door opened and Ronan's mother stood back to allow him room to enter.

"Braden, you are home. Please come in. How were your travels?" she asked, offering him a chair at their table. She was alone, and he could tell she'd been crying. Her husband had died two years ago and Ronan's two younger brothers, Keith and Moray, were probably at the lists practicing.

"It was a nice journey south. We attended a Drummond wedding, which was lovely."

Her shoulders drooped and she sighed raggedly. "A wedding, something Ronan and Marta would have been celebrating in a few moons, if only…"

As much as it might upset her, he had to ask questions, the same ones that had been preying on his mind for the entire journey south. "Have you learned aught about that day? Has Marta revealed who she was speaking with?"

"Marta is saying verra little. She cries and carries on, so I do not ask her anymore." Tears slid down her cheeks while she talked. "Mayhap go to the lists, talk to Ronan's brothers. 'Twas one of the lads who told me Marta was carrying on with another." She paused to stare up at the ceiling, perplexed. "Or was it Ronan himself?"

Braden decided not to continue pestering the woman since all he seemed to do was bring back painful memories. "Is there something I can do for you? I know Ronan did many things to help out. Do you need wood chopped? May I get you some stew for dinner tonight? I'm sure Cook would have extra."

"Braden, you are kind to think of an old woman, but I've been cooking to keep my mind off Ronan. His brothers have been cutting wood daily. I think it helps them to keep busy. Thank you, but we are not in need of anything. You are part of the laird's family. You have more important duties to tend to." She patted his hand and he decided to leave since he could think of nothing else to offer her in her grief. The only thing he could do to truly help was find more answers, and he would not stop until he was sure. He said goodbye and headed toward the lists, surprised to see the large number of guards there today. On the morrow, he'd be taking a few of these men to Muir land, his first mission that he'd be leading.

"Keith!" After several minutes of searching, he finally found Keith sparring with his younger brother, Moray. They both stopped when they saw Braden, stepping out of the practice area to speak with him.

"You fare well, Braden?" Keith asked, clapping him on the shoulder.

"Aye. How are you lads doing? I find I still miss Ronan." He couldn't hide the truth of the matter. Being away had helped him focus his thoughts elsewhere, but now that he was home, the wound left by his friend's absence felt as fresh as it had on the day of Ronan's death.

"We miss him, too." Moray ran a hand down his face, wiping the sweat he'd accumulated from his brow.

"Any news?"

"About what?" Moray asked. "Ronan threw himself over the cliff because he thought Marta had found someone new. What else could there be? We're done trying to find out why Ronan did what he did, Braden. As of late, we've rather been trying to find peace."

Braden shuffled his feet. "Ronan's death continues to perplex me. Has Marta revealed who the lad was? Is she seeing anyone now?"

"Nay," Keith said, grabbing a skin and taking a long swig. "She says she loved Ronan and I believe her. Och, she did say one thing. She said the only other lad she spoke with that day was you, Braden."

Moray jerked his head around and gave Braden a strange look. "Do you recall speaking with her? Or anything unusual in her demeanor?"

Braden thought hard, almost ready to shake his head, but then something popped into his memory. "I wouldn't exactly say we spoke that day, but I do recall passing her on the way to the lists. She dropped her basket and I helped her pick up the items and put them back. Mostly sewing things. But we barely spoke."

"Do you think my brother could have misconstrued your conversation?" Keith suggested.

Braden snorted, his hands settling on his hips. "Nay. There was naught to be suspicious about. Is that what you're thinking? That it was me who became entangled with Marta?"

Moray glanced at Keith, who shrugged his shoulders. "We'll never know, will we?"

Braden ignored his suggestion. It was ridiculous and surely did not warrant further discussion. Ronan would never have resorted to such a desperate action over such a little thing. And had Ronan suspected him, he would have given him an earful, and probably a fistful, himself. They were practically brothers.

"That's not what I came here to talk about. I came to

ask if the two of you would like to go on a patrol with me on the morrow. We're traveling southwest toward Buchan land and a few others to see if they have been inhabited by anyone. My uncle prefers to be aware of all neighbors. We may travel for a day or two, mayhap more. But before you agree, let it be said that if either of you don't believe what I've told you about my involvement with Marta, then you don't belong in my group."

Moray sighed, then said, "Aye, I believe you, Braden. I know how close you were with Ronan. I just still get protective about him. Forgive me."

Keith said, "Moray's right. I trust you, and I'd be honored to go along with you."

Moray nodded. "I'll be there. My thanks, Braden. 'Tis best to keep busy, I've found."

"Accepted. Roddy and I will see you at dawn. I'll gather another ten guards to come along with us."

Keith clasped his shoulder and said, "My thanks. We'd better practice our sword skills a wee bit more."

The two returned to the lists and Braden found himself thinking again about Ronan and Marta. He could not imagine committing such a rash act over a lass. Even so, he and Roddy and Connor were all of marriageable age, something he'd thought of often since his cousin David's wedding. He'd never even considered marriage until then.

He couldn't. He'd made a bargain with himself, and he intended to see it through. Had he been paying attention to Ronan, he would have noticed his depression, seen how much he was hurting or in need of someone to talk with. But he hadn't. He'd been unable to save his friend, so he'd promised his Lord he'd make up for that failure.

He had to save two others. It did not matter who they were or why.

It was his new purpose for his life. Two for one.

CHAPTER FOUR

———◆———

CAIRSTINE PLACED A SOFT PILLOW on the bench
for Steenie to sit on for the midday meal. It was a
sennight after he'd gotten lost, and he'd angered Greer yet
again. He was pouting, but she ignored him, patting the
pillow for him to take a seat. The lad's uncle came into the
hall, whistling, but he stopped when he saw Steenie settling down gingerly. A wicked grin plastered across Blair's
face, and Cairstine wished she had the courage to slap it
off.

"Steenie still have a sore arse? Has it not been quite a
while since you had your arse whipped by my brother?"

Steenie fought his tears. "Nay."

Blair reached for the pillow. "Och, 'tis been long enough.
Toss that pillow aside, act like a man."

Steenie fought to keep the pillow. "Nay!"

Blair quirked his brow at Cairstine, his grin fading.
"Another one?"

Cairstine gave him a wee nod, hoping Steenie wouldn't
see her. The lad had been through enough.

"What did you do this time?"

"Naught. Leave me be, Uncle Blair." Steenie stared at the
table, holding the pillow on both sides so it would not be
pulled out from under him.

Cairstine thought Blair was the kinder of the two, when
it came to brutal killers. Sometimes she wondered what

their childhood had been like, what had made them the way they are. Apparently, their sire had been a cruel man, but Cairstine knew little about their past since both of their parents had passed on years ago. They never talked about their family, and she never willingly conversed with them about anything.

The door flew open again and Greer entered. A grin grew on his face as soon as his gaze landed on Steenie.

"Good day to you, Papa," Steenie said quietly.

"You still sitting on that pillow?" his father said as a greeting. How Cairstine hated his cruelty to the wee lad.

"What did you do to him this time, Greer?" Blair asked. "He's in a mood as if he just took a beating."

"I whipped his arse for sitting on that pillow for too long. I told him if he needed the pillow so badly, I'd give him a reason to need it."

Steenie fought his tears. "Papa, I've been good."

Greer moved over and grabbed the pillow out from under him. Steenie gave a brief howl, but he immediately quieted himself, staring at his sire with a fear that wrenched Cairstine's heart. "Sit without a pillow. Your mother needs to stop coddling you. Or do you need another arse whipping?"

"Nay, I'll sit without it." Steenie said, his voice higher pitched than usual because of the pain he was bearing.

Cairstine decided it was time to speak her mind. Greer was often tamed a bit by his brother's presence. "Why must you be so cruel, Greer? He's only a lad."

Greer reached over and grabbed her plait, yanking her off the bench. "I'll do as I like, and you'll keep your mouth shut."

"I'd take better care of you, Cairstine. Leave him and be mine." Blair gave her a bright smile, his eyes gleaming the way they always did whenever he taunted his older brother. Greer was two years older than Blair. He waggled his eyebrows at her, but she didn't answer.

As if she'd be with either of them by choice.

"Papa, leave Mama be. I'll take her punishment," Steenie said bravely.

"Laddie, nay," Cairstine whispered, her feet nearly leaving the ground because of the pain shooting through her head. Greer still had not released her hair.

"Then bend yourself over the bench, Steenie," the *bastart* scoffed. "I'll be happy to give you her punishment. Maybe you'll stop acting like such a lassie."

To her surprise, Blair did something he'd never done before. He defended them. "Let her go and leave your wee son alone."

Greer released her hair and stepped close enough to his brother to spit in his face. When they stood nose to nose, he ground out, "What did you say?"

Blair didn't budge. "I said leave them be. You've hurt both of them enough for this moon. I'm tired of watching your cruelty."

"*My* cruelty? This pronouncement from the lad who cuts his enemies down without a care? Your blood is far colder than mine, brother, and well you know it."

Blair shook his head. "Don't compare yourself to me. I don't hurt women the way you do. I appreciate their finer qualities. And if I had a son, I'd take better care of him, too. I wish I had someone to take care of me when I grow old. But the way you treat them, they'll leave you as soon as they're able."

Cairstine had never heard such a conversation between the brothers. She sat down next to Steenie, and he leaned into her to hide his tears.

"You want them both?"

The two stared at each other, and you could have heard the drop of a needle in the hall. The servants and the guards who'd just entered all froze, waiting to see what would happen.

This was a new event for all of them.

Cairstine held her breath, unable to believe Greer had just offered her and Steenie to his brother.

The door burst open and two more guards flew across the floor to stand opposite the brothers, their eyes widening when they noticed the tense situation between the two men.

"What is it?" Greer asked, not moving a muscle beyond the ones in his jaw. "And it needs to be mighty important or I'll beat you both until you'll not swive for days."

"Problem, my lord. There's a group of Grant warriors headed our way."

The brothers broke their silent standoff to turn toward the guards.

"What?" Blair asked in surprise.

Greer acted as though he'd been hit by the blade of a sword, jumping and moving away from his brother. "How many? And how do you know they're Grants?"

"They're wearing the Grant plaid and carrying the Grant banner. Less than twenty, but more than a dozen."

Greer headed out the door and shouted. "All guards are to take up posts near the gates." The dozen or so in the hall bolted out of their seats to follow him. Then he mumbled, "What the hell could they want? They've never bothered us before. And where the hell are the rest of our men?"

Blair said, "Calm down, Greer. The men are practicing in the fields. The Grants never suspected any wrong of us many years ago, and they don't now. We stayed away long enough after the attack to allay any suspicion that could be cast our way. They've got naught to be concerned about."

Greer gave his brother a small nod. "You're probably right, but check the cellars first. Then be out by the gates. I have a feeling this isn't about being neighborly."

Cairstine grabbed Steenie and hurried toward the back door. Her sire had always taught her and her brother to hide by the small entrance in the back wall of the castle. If fighting started, they were to take off. Of course, they hadn't listened to his instructions when it mattered most and look what had transpired because of their mistake.

Greer bellowed, "Steenie, you're coming with me. Time for you to learn how to be a man. You'll stay with the guards on the wall. Cairstine, I care not what the hell you do, but stay out of the bailey."

Her heart raced. She hated to be pulled away from her son, but she knew Greer would not allow anything different. Steenie hugged her leg, and she didn't have the heart to push him away. "Greer, he's only five winters. He could be hurt."

"I said stop coddling him. Do you wish to keep arguing? Shall I thrash him again for you when this is done?"

Hell, how she hated the way he used Steenie to force her into submission. "Go with Papa. He'll take care of you. Go."

Fortunately, Steenie took off behind his sire and Blair, his mouth starting with his questions. "Is there to be a battle, Uncle Blair? Will it be a bad one?"

She loved how the lad could adjust to nearly every situation. He had to, or he'd never survive being a Lamont.

For herself, she was heading out the back, just as her sire had taught her.

———◆———

BRADEN, CONNOR, AND RODDY LED the group of five and ten Grant warriors toward Muir land. They'd traveled all the way south to Buchan land and not found any evidence of the Lamonts or of Cairstine and her son. He prayed they'd find them soon. He'd seen women nearly beaten to death by men such as Greer Lamont.

"Have you been anywhere near here of late?" Braden asked his cousin.

"Nay," Roddy replied, spitting off to the side of his horse. "Damn midges. Will they never quit?" He scratched his head in response to the annoying insects. "Not surprised you volunteered for this duty. You think she'll be here?"

Braden hadn't been able to get her out of his mind. Hell-fire, she had stirred him something fierce. "I wouldn't be upset if I found her, but if she's married to the bastard, there's not much I can do."

"Think you she could be Muir's daughter? Once I gave that possibility serious consideration, I began to believe 'tis exactly what we could find here. Would that change your mind?" Roddy asked, slapping at the midges again.

Braden sighed. "Aye, 'twould probably give me a stronger drive to go after Lamont. If she's a Muir, I doubt she went with them willingly." Hell, he hoped not.

Connor said, "Never know. Women can be strange about things. How do you wish to do this since you're in charge? Just go to the front gate? We don't have enough men to attack if we *do* find the Lamonts are in residence. If that bastard is here with her, don't go charging at him. We may not be able to back you up. We have no idea how many men are in his guard. 'Tis one of the primary reasons we're here—to uncover who occupies the castle and how many."

"Why would you say that? I can control my temper." True, he'd lost his temper on occasion, but he'd never hurt anyone without just cause. The issue at the Drummond's hadn't been that memorable, and the fool had deserved it. True, he'd gotten himself in trouble a few times, but he'd never hurt anyone but himself. And the only person he'd truly managed to pish off was his own da.

"I saw you at the Drummond keep, remember?" Roddy smirked, glancing at him.

"I'll control myself." His mind raced with a hundred different scenarios, but most of them ended the same way. He doubted he'd see the lass if they didn't get past the gate, and if the Lamonts had taken the castle after all, he doubted he'd get inside. He wouldn't be satisfied if the brothers came to the gates and sent them away. He'd know they were here, but what good would that do him if he could not learn aught about her?

He had to find out the truth. Was she here willingly?

"If 'tis possible that she is there, with the Lamonts, I'd like the chance to come in through the back, see how they are living. How are they supporting themselves? Feeding their people?"

"If there is a back entrance."

"Allow me to approach the castle from the back. If there's no door in the curtain wall, I'll sneak in from behind while their guards are up front. I can't explain myself, but something was not right between those two. I need to see how they really live." Braden had wanted to beat the man to a pulp, and not for disrespecting him. "The people in the huts south of here think this place is occupied, and we've found no evidence of the Lamonts elsewhere. They have to be living here. None of the people we visited wished to talk about Muir Castle, as if 'tis haunted. Mayhap 'tis not inhabited by ghosts but by vicious men."

Roddy asked, "And you think you can come between Lamont and his lass? Many men mistreat their wives. My da says my mama was grossly mistreated when he found her. You know about Aunt Maddie and your mother. 'Tis common outside Grant walls."

Braden snorted. "And all three of those men are now dead. Cruelty doesn't happen on our land. And I'd be glad to make the Lamonts another example of that rule."

Roddy thought on that for a moment and nodded. "Agreed. If you want to come in through the back, 'tis fine with me. We'll approach the front gates. Do you want any men with you?"

"Nay. I'll be quick about it. If they are there, I'll get inside, do a wee bit of spy business and be on my way." Even if he saw her, would he be able to speak with her? "I only ask that you question them at the gates as to how long they've been living in Muir Castle."

Connor said, "They won't admit they know it's Muir

Castle if they are guilty of massacring the clan."

"But ask. Someone standing at the gates may give away a truth without realizing it. Be subtle."

"Aye, we'll see it done the way you want," Roddy replied.

Braden was glad he had Roddy's agreement. Uncle Alex had put him in charge of this scouting mission, so he didn't need his cousins' permission, but he was grateful to have it. It confirmed his was a sound plan, not just driven by his need to see the lass.

He did his best to convince himself of that. He simply couldn't get this close without finding out the truth of the matter.

"Suits me."

Braden pulled away from the group before the gates came into view.

He found a place to tie off his horse, dismounted, and crept toward the back of the curtain wall. The castle was much smaller than Grant Castle, and though it was well built, it clearly was not well cared for. There were three towers, one with living quarters, and a sound curtain wall for protection. The first thing he noticed was the smell of meat cooking. The kitchens were in use. That could only mean one thing.

Someone was living here. How he hoped it was the Lamonts.

And Cairstine.

CHAPTER FIVE

TEARS THREATENED TO FLOOD CAIRSTINE'S cheeks. The old fear of an attack clawed at her throat. Six years ago, she'd lived it. She remembered the fear she'd heard in her mother's voice, the trembling of her sire's hand on her back as he urged her and her brother to hide upstairs instead of going out the back while he fought bravely alongside warriors.

Massacred, all of them.

Would this be another massacre? A part of her could wish for retribution for her clan, but her focus was on her son. She said a quick prayer to protect her wee lad. The man she'd met near Drummond land had said he was a Grant. Were they coming to find her? In all the four years since the Lamonts had returned to her home they'd done their best to destroy, no one had thought to inquire on the property to her knowledge. Why would they now?

She fought the dread deep in her heart over what was about to happen, rubbing her forehead in the hopes of pulling something from the depths of her memory about the Grants. She would cling to the small hope that this could be good, just as Corc had predicted. The Grants, or at least the ones in the red plaids the other night, seemed honorable. When her sire was alive, he often talked about the strongest clans, and the Grants were among them.

A fleeting glimpse popped into her mind, of a very tall

man in a red plaid carrying his daughter up on his shoulders while she giggled. He had dark hair and looked much like two of the warriors she'd seen on Drummond land.

The man that had followed her outside the Drummond gates had a similar appearance. Had that been his sire?

If this turned out to be Braden Grant's clan, it could be a blessing.

But the Lamonts would fight the Grants if provoked. She hoped they brought enough reinforcements if their intentions were good.

Please, God, keep Steenie out of harm's way. Spare him. He's a good boy.

Tears pricked her eyes. What reason would she have to live if she lost her son? How she prayed she would never be forced to experience such a tragedy. After she opened the hidden door in the curtain wall, she peered out before she progressed down the path, swinging at all the brush falling in her face. Her sire had always kept the path trimmed just in case they needed to run, but Greer and Blair couldn't be bothered with such things. Once she had volunteered to clear the path herself, but she'd been promptly reminded she was not to step outside the curtain wall alone.

She didn't hear any loud shouts or war whoops, but her fear made her less than cautious, so much so that she hurried down a fork in the path without noticing the man standing in the large oak trees until he reached out and grabbed her, pulling her close.

She swung her fists, frustrated that she'd been so careless. "Leave me be. You have no right to touch me." In her mind, he was Greer, and this was the day he'd caught her running six years ago.

"Lass, I'll not hurt you. Stop, please. I'll set you free if you promise not to scream." His voice stayed her because it sounded warm and familiar.

It occurred to her that although the man held her tight in his muscular arms, he possessed a gentleness she'd never experienced with Greer. Whereas her captor had a brutal, punishing grip, this man made her instantly melt to his form and feel that she'd be safe. Once that realization struck her, she stopped fighting and lifted her gaze to his.

She released a little gasp. This was Braden Grant, the one who she'd begged with her eyes to find her again.

He'd followed her once already to see if she was hale, knowing Greer had slapped her. And now here he was again, though she wasn't sure what his intentions were this time. She'd learned a long time ago not to hold out hope or trust the greedy nature of men.

She stared into Braden's eyes, neither of them speaking as they took each other's measure. Her muscles loosened against him, and she felt strangely comforted by his arms instead of threatened by them. But she wouldn't completely let herself relent yet; she had her laddie to protect. "What do you want this time?"

His eyes were the color of chestnuts, a warm brown that drew her in, and he looked even more handsome than he had that day at the festival. A strong jawline with a bit of dark stubble, just enough to tempt her to touch his cheek. His long hair curled at his neck, a beautiful shade of light brown she'd not seen before. If he stood in the sun, she guessed she'd see gold strands threaded through the brown. A small scar on his chin did not detract from his looks at all, but rather, gave him a look of rugged boyishness.

"Who are you?" his husky voice sent a strange feeling through her middle, almost a shiver, but that made no sense.

The only men she'd trusted had belonged to Clan Muir. She wouldn't tell him anything until she could be sure of her safety. "I'll have your answer first. You're on my clan's land." She lifted her chin a notch. "Why are you here?"

"I'm here in the name of my laird, Alexander Grant. Are you saying you're a surviving member of the Muir clan?"

He was correct in his assumption. This was Muir land, not Lamont land. And if she could find a way to reclaim it for the Muirs, she would do so without fail to make her sire proud. Indeed, she'd thought of nothing but vengeance immediately after her capture, but the thoughts had since slipped away. What a foolish idea to think one lass could go up against the Lamont brothers. Hadn't she learned the truth the day she'd tried to run away with Steenie?

As Braden turned his head for a moment, she caught sight of his eyelashes, the thickest and longest she'd ever seen on a man. And his eyes held the promise of respect. Was it possible that he could assist her?

She pushed against his chest, surprised by how hard and powerful it felt. Her inclination was to trust him. To tell him everything, but she knew that was foolish because she couldn't risk the one thing that mattered to her.

Steenie.

A summer ago, she'd tried to run away, sneaking out the back with Steenie when he'd been asleep in her arms. Corc had left a horse for her at the back, and she'd crept out in the middle of the night, leading her horse away as fast as she could.

She'd been frightened by the sounds of wolves, by the wild boar she'd seen in the distance, but she'd moved on, hopeful that if she could get to one of her neighbors, they would protect her.

Her horse had tired and they'd never made it off Muir land. How Greer had discovered her absence, she'd never know. When he'd caught up with them, he'd pulled her from her horse and beaten her while Steenie cried. When he'd finished with her, leaving her sore and collapsed on the ground in a huddled mess, he'd held Steenie up in front of her.

"Shall I beat him while you watch, Cairstine? And I don't mean thrash him. I'll use my fists this time." The fury she'd seen on his face had frightened her more than anything.

"Nay, please, Greer. I'm sorry. Please don't hurt him. He's only four." She'd fought to stand but had crumpled on a bruised ankle.

"You try to leave me again, and I'll beat him until he's a bloody pulp. Do you hear me, wench?"

"Aye. I promise! Please don't beat him." She'd made it up on her knees, sobbing and begging Greer to leave the lad alone.

Then he'd handed Steenie over to Blair and tossed her over his horse, mounting behind her.

He had never said another word to her until he put her in the locked room in the cellar. Before he left, he turned to her and said, "Next time, I'll kill you, but not before I beat Steenie while you watch. Then I'll sell him across the waters to live the life of a servant."

She'd vowed never to run away again. While dying didn't matter to her—in fact, it might be a relief from her dark life—watching her son beaten did, and the thought of him being sold frightened her more than anything. Where would he end up?

To her disappointment, Braden loosened his grip on her. His finger reached for her chin, lifting her gaze to his. "I see the pain in your eyes, and I swear to banish that look forever if you'd trust me."

Partly in shock from his words, she stepped away. No one but Corc had shown her an ounce of care or compassion over the last six years. She did her best to quell the hope that bloomed in her heart at the possibility that his words were true.

He surprised her even more when he said, "You needn't move away. I quite like you there, and I won't allow him to slap you again like he did on Drummond land. You're the reason I'm here. I came looking for you."

Her gaze darted to his. Ah, so he did remember her. Could he be telling the truth? Would he have come here just for her? Confusion clouded her mind. Men in battle didn't think about women.

"Men do not hit women in my clan." Braden Grant persisted. "Tell me, lass, is Greer Lamont your husband?"

"Nay!" Her quick reply almost came out in a shout, but she squelched it in time. "Nay," she whispered, "we are not married."

Braden let out a breath he'd been holding. He hadn't realized how much he'd wanted her *not* to be married to a Lamont. "Your name?"

"Cairstine."

"Are you his sister?" She was more beautiful than she'd appeared at the Drummonds. The thick golden plait of her hair fell forward over her shoulder nearly to her waist, and a few freckles dotted the bridge of her nose. And yet her green eyes were wells of fear. While she had every right to be wary of him, he wished to convince her that he was trustworthy, that there were honorable men in the world. "Or are you a Muir?"

Being this close to her, taking in her sweet floral scent, stirred his loins in a way he wished to control. This was not the time. He'd enjoyed holding her in his arms, her soft breasts touching his chest in a way that would undoubtedly haunt his dreams in the nights to come, but perhaps it was better that they now had distance between them. It allowed him to think, something he couldn't do with her rosy lips just a touch beneath his own.

Perhaps it would be better to leave her be, but he couldn't. He repeated his question because she'd given him a blank stare as though she had to think about her answer. "Are you his sister?"

"Nay," she shook her head, a look of confusion crossing her face.

He waited for her to give him more information about why she was with the Lamonts, but she said nothing, so he pushed her. "Are you the surviving daughter of the Muir? Were you taken captive by the Lamonts several years ago?"

She blushed and nodded. "Aye. How I wish the answer were different."

"Why do you stay?" He'd take her with him now, get her safely away from the brute; if that's what she wanted, that was. He cared not if the Lamont men did not like it. He'd fight them for her.

"You know why. My son. I love him."

"But I'll protect you." His finger reached up and caressed her cheek. "You do not deserve to be treated as I've seen him treat you. The Lamonts are murderers, are they not? Did they not kill your parents? My clan will bring them to justice. Come with me now, and I'll see you are safe. I'll come back for your son."

The tears she'd been struggling to hide erupted as if she'd held them inside for decades. "I can't. You don't know what he'd do. I tried to run away before, and he…he…"

His hand reached for her neck, massaging her soft skin gently. "Hush, you have nothing to fear from me, and I promise to see this situation righted. He'll never hurt you again. Clan Grant has over five hundred warriors. We can handle the Lamonts."

"But Steenie…he said…"

She leaned into him, clutching his tunic as she cried into his shoulder.

Braden whispered, "What did he say? You can tell me."

She gulped, and he held her, surprised at how a sudden calm overwhelmed him, as if he were meant to hold her exactly where she was. He closed his eyes and inhaled her scent, a sweetness to her unlike anything he'd ever known.

She managed to pull back enough to gaze into his eyes. "He said he would kill me and sell Steenie across the water…"

Braden couldn't help but be startled about the mention of selling a child. Could the Lamonts be involved with the Channel of Dubh? Did they know of it? All sorts of possibilities battled in his mind. What to do first?

First, he had to get her and her son to safety.

A harsh voice called to her from the door in the curtain

wall. "Cairstine? Where the hell are you?"

"Hush," she whispered. "I think 'twas Greer."

He took hold of her hand, caressing the tender skin on the back, and said, "Come with me. I'll take you away from him."

She tugged her hand away and whispered, "Nay. I cannot." She stepped away from him, but he took ahold of her wrist.

"Stay. Trust me to take you away from here and make sure he never hurts you again. I'll talk to my laird about helping you regain the land that is rightfully yours, and we'll come back for Steenie. I'll get you to my warriors and return for him in less than an hour, but I must get you away first."

He could see the briefest glint of hope in her eyes before she turned away. "I must not leave without him. Let me be." Her voice and her eyes didn't support her words. The way she held her body told him she'd softened toward him, maybe even wanted to join him, but the thought of Greer selling their son clearly held her back. He released her, though every bit of him wanted to sweep her away to safety. At the same time, he recalled Connor's warning that they hadn't brought enough men to stand up in a battle against the Lamonts. This was merely a mission for information with strict instructions from Uncle Alex, and to act rashly could risk his ability to save her and her son. And he swore he would. He counted on his cousins to discover the true number of guards they held here.

As he watched her retreating back, he tried to piece it together. She'd admitted that Greer had taken her captive, and her voice had nearly broken when she'd expressed her wish to break free.

Well, he'd offered her the perfect chance to escape and she'd rejected him. But how could he blame her when Lamont had threatened to kill her and do the unthinkable with her son?

Braden had almost reached his horse when a small voice called down from the curtain wall. "Mama? Mama, where are you?"

Braden climbed atop his horse and glanced over at the curtain wall before he left, watching as a young lad charged up to Cairstine and hugged her. Greer stood next to the door, observing the reunion without participating in it.

Everything became clear to Braden in an instant. His sire had said the Muirs had been attacked five or six years ago, just about the age of the wee laddie. Cairstine hadn't admitted they'd killed her parents, but what else could have happened? They'd laid low and disappeared when his sire had sent his warriors here. She'd said how she wished her situation were different.

Braden's life had just changed unequivocally, irrevocably in a way he'd never anticipated. The knowledge he'd gained from this scouting visit would have a lasting effect on him. Greer Lamont hadn't just massacred Cairstine Muir's clan.

When he and his brother had finished murdering her family, he'd raped and abducted her.

By his honor as a Grant, he'd avenge her clan and her treatment by the Lamonts. Soon enough, this life would be dead to Cairstine.

Because Greer Lamont was a dead man.

CHAPTER SIX

B RADEN FLICKED THE REINS OF his horse, heading back toward the path where he'd left Roddy and
Connor before traveling behind the curtain wall. He could
see the group heading back toward Grant land. He'd found
exactly what he'd hoped to find, the answers to so many
of his questions.

He called out to his cousin. "Roddy, what did you learn?"

"Not much," he replied. "The Lamont brothers are definitely in control, but they claim the castle was abandoned
when they overtook it four years ago. They denied killing the Muirs, said they knew naught of them; that they'd
deserted their castle south of here and come upon this one
empty. Had no idea whose castle it was, just assumed since
much of it was ruined that they could inhabit it."

"No doubt a lie." Killers and rapists also tended to be
liars.

"Could be. They claim they come and go as they please,
don't bother anyone and don't want any trouble. The place
looks as if it's deteriorated under their watch, though 'tis
difficult to tell from the outside with the curtain wall
intact. The outside huts are mostly in shambles. Muir sup-
ported a clan here from what Uncle Alex said, yet there is
little that speaks of a prosperous group. I got a glimpse at
a few of the cottages inside, but they haven't been kept up.
There are no crops being planted as far as I could tell. How

do they survive?"

"Did anyone get inside?" he asked, hoping for a wee bit more information.

"Nay. We just spoke to them at the gates. Offered assistance as good neighbors, but we were refused. My guess is they are the reivers we've noted on and off over the last four years. They'd have no other way of supporting themselves."

"How many guards?"

Roddy held his horse back and tipped his head to Ronan's brothers. "Lads, did you get any count on the guards? Either of you?"

"I saw around a dozen," Keith said.

"Aye," Moray added, "and twenty to thirty in the lists."

"So they can't have more than fifty," Braden said. He couldn't stop a smile from crossing his face at the thought of storming Muir Castle and retaliating against the murderous brothers.

Roddy nodded to Keith and Moray and then pulled up ahead of them as they moved through a narrow part of the trail. Braden rode directly ahead of his cousins. The clouds above were gray, though it hadn't rained on them yet. They picked their way across the path carefully, avoiding the muddy areas, and moved slow enough to comfortably converse.

Once they were out of Keith and Moray's hearing, Roddy asked, "Why does that please you? What did you discover behind the curtain wall? We saw no lasses at all."

Connor said, "Speak up, Braden. You look as though you've swallowed a bird that's fighting to get out."

Braden glanced back. "I found what I was searching for," he said with a smirk.

Roddy looked stunned, turning around to make sure they couldn't be overheard. "A certain lass?"

"Aye, a beautiful lass named Cairstine Muir. And she gave me a clue as to why they don't have any fields producing.

They don't need them."

"Hellfire." Roddy let out a low whistle. "She is a Muir. Married to one of the Lamonts?"

"Nay. She was taken captive." He pursed his lips to keep himself from cursing and sharing what he planned to do to the doomed brothers.

"God's teeth," Roddy whispered. "Why did you not bring her with you?"

Braden said, "I tried, but she refused. Her son was not with her, but with Greer Lamont. She won't leave the laddie behind."

"Did the Lamonts kill her clan?" Connor asked.

"She didn't say nay."

"What the hell does that mean?" Connor asked.

"I was about to ask her that question directly, but we were interrupted."

"Stop speaking in riddles and tell us all you learned," Connor barked. Braden could often see Uncle Alex in Connor's ways. Neither of them was patient when it came to dealing with bastards.

"Here's what I know. She is a Muir who'd been taken captive by the Lamonts. She has a son of five winters. The reason she doesn't leave is because she tried to escape a year ago, but Greer caught her and beat her, then promised if she ever did it again, he'd sell her son over the water…"

"He raped her and got her with child?" Roddy shouted.

"Over the water? As in the Channel of Dubh?" Connor's wide-eyed gaze stared at both him and Roddy.

"Aye, 'tis the word I would use, Roddy. And Connor, I think 'tis possible that across the water does indeed mean the Channel of Dubh."

"Is it Greer who attacked her? Or his brother, or both?" Connor added.

Braden squeezed his eyes shut at the thought of the two brothers… "Don't ever mention the possibility of both of them again."

Connor tipped his head toward Roddy. "I think we have a new mission. 'Tis time to send someone for Will and Maggie."

"So, she fears for her life and her son's. Either way, Braden," Roddy said quietly so no one would overhear. "She refused to come with you. I'm glad you did not force her. Think you she would be willing if you guarantee her safety?"

Braden glanced at the treetops overhead as they traveled through the heavily forested area. His cousins were his closest friends and usually they were also quite in tune to his thoughts, but this time they did not fully understand.

The pine branches waved as the wind picked up. It occurred to him that he was acting completely out of character. He should be furious, ranting wildly, cursing revenge on the brothers, and promising to kill them with his own sword. But something in him had changed. He felt angry, aye, but he also felt *calm*. The same way he'd felt with Cairstine in his arms. He didn't need to speak his vow because it had become a part of him, a driving force to be reckoned with.

The Lamonts would not stop him. He knew that like he knew his own name.

"Braden, what's wrong?"

"Naught. All is well," he said, glancing back. "I've already promised her that I'll protect her and her son, but please keep this between us until we talk to our laird."

Roddy's eyes widened and he drew his horse closer to Braden's mount. "You know Uncle Alex will support you. But we must wait until we have enough warriors. They have at least fifty. We must have more. You have no doubt this is what you wish to do?"

Braden nodded because he'd never been more sure of anything. "I spoke with her, actually held her in my arms for a moment, but we were interrupted. One of the Lamonts yelled her name…and then the young lad called out for his mother."

"And?" Connor asked.

"And I witnessed her fear firsthand. She ran as soon as Lamont called to her, but she didn't want to. Had the lad been with us, I may have been able to make off with the both of them that instant. Make clear, though, Connor, I'll not stop until I get her and the laddie away from that bastard."

He shifted his gaze back to his cousin.

"You have my support, cousin." He stopped his horse for a second, staring at Braden in expectation.

"Nay, not now," Braden whispered. "We do not have the men, and Greer is not going anywhere. She'll be there on the morrow. But we must make haste. We don't want this visit to tip the Lamonts off that we'll be back again and give them an opportunity to slip through our grasp."

"What are you planning?" Roddy moved his horse forward.

"First we go to our sires and our laird, and if they will not assist us, then we'll summon our Band of Cousins. From what Cairstine said, there could be an even bigger operation that needs our attention; this could involve the Channel. The Grants will want to be involved."

Roddy thought for a moment and then nodded, chewing on his lower lip in anger. "I agree."

They cleared the forest into a meadow, now full of spring and early summer wildflowers. Braden flicked the reins of his horse and took the animal into a gallop, the Highland breeze rippling through his long hair. The wind in his face reminded him of something he had that Cairstine did not.

Freedom.

"MAMA! YOU SHOULD HAVE COME with us!" Steenie's excitement bubbled over. "I saw them. The Grants. Have you never seen them? They were the biggest and strongest warriors I've ever seen. They all wear red plaids." His eyes shone with enthusiasm she hadn't seen from him in a while. "They wore the same plaid as that other man."

"What other man?" Greer tipped his chin toward the place she'd been standing. "Was he not the same as the warrior on Drummond land?"

"I ran to hide from another attack. I had no idea he would be there," she replied, not wanting to lie to Greer for fear he'd beat an answer out of her. "He said he was a Grant."

Greer grabbed her by her plait and yanked her close.

"Ow, Greer. That hurts." She stood on her tiptoes in an attempt to lessen the pain. "I did not invite him here."

"If I ever catch you with another man…" he ground out. "You won't like it."

"Papa, don't hurt Mama. Please?" Steenie grabbed her hand.

She focused on Steenie—his voice, his eyes, the feel of his soft skin against hers. It was the best way to deal with whatever pain Greer inflicted on her. She vowed not to upset her son, no matter what it took.

He was the only thing that mattered anymore.

"Steenie, return to the keep," Greer said.

Steenie did as he was told. He had already learned not to argue with a beast; he would only get beaten. But he didn't first leave without saying, in his sweet voice, "I love you, Mama."

"I said go! Now!" Greer's face contorted, his features turning deep red as his fury blossomed.

"Go inside, Steenie. Mama will be fine." Cairstine did her best to convince the sweet lad that she was hale. She just wanted him to go before Greer's temper turned in his direction. She should have left with the man, but she'd chosen to stay. There'd been no other choice with Steenie near the wall. What more did Greer want from her?

Once Steenie disappeared, Greer brought his face close to hers. "Did I see you next to that Grant warrior? It looked as though you were mighty close to him when I first saw you," he growled.

"He grabbed me against my will. Please, Greer, loosen your grip." She closed her eyes, not wanting to even look at the *bastart*.

"I think you need a wee lesson to remind you who you belong to. You're mine. Do not ever think otherwise. A thousand Grant warriors won't be able to take you from me or keep me from finding you." He yanked her plait, pulling her toward the keep. Once inside, he dragged her toward the stairway to the cellars.

"I can't keep up with you going down the stairs, Greer. You're going too fast." She stumbled and fell against him, but he shoved her upright.

"There's a fine chamber for you down here, somewhere you can learn to remember who your master is." He opened a door and threw her inside, letting go of her hair at the last moment.

Cairstine let out a yelp in pain, unable to hold it in any longer. She stumbled and fell to the ground, twisting her ankle in the process. She glanced up at the *bastart*, hoping he would just leave her alone.

He stood over her. "If you ever try to leave me, I'll come after you and kill you, as I've warned you before. You need to remember that, wench. You'll never get away from me." He stepped back into the passageway and closed the door, turning the key in the lock. There was a window in the door with four bars inside. She'd tried to take inventory of this place when he'd thrown her in here before, though she'd been barely conscious most of the time. If it weren't for Steenie, she'd rather live in this cold, damp place because it meant fewer occasions to run into Greer.

Her sire had never needed to take any prisoners, but the brothers kept three chambers for that purpose alone. She hadn't known of an occasion that they'd needed to lock anyone away besides her. The very thought of keeping prisoners made her skin crawl.

Once she heard Greer's retreating footsteps, she sat up, massaging her scalp. Glancing around the dark chamber, she found the pallet against the far wall and a pot in the corner. She climbed onto the pallet and collapsed into sobs.

How she wished she'd gone with Braden Grant. Though he'd promised to return for her, she'd learned long ago not to underestimate the Lamonts' ability to take away the one thing she had.

Hope.

CHAPTER SEVEN

—————•—————

UPON RETURNING TO GRANT CASTLE, Braden, Connor, and Roddy immediately sought out an audience with their sires and Uncle Alex.

Once they were all settled in the solar, Uncle Alex asked, "What did you discover, lads?

Connor started. "Oh, it's something you'll want to hear, Uncle. There was no one at Buchan Castle, it's still deserted. There were five of the king's guards there to keep reivers away. They knew naught about the Lamonts. We didn't find anything else until we traveled to our last stop, Muir Castle."

Braden pursed his lips. "And there, we found the answers to our questions and more."

"Did you bring the lass with you, get her away from the bastards?" his sire asked.

"Nay," Roddy said. "The Lamonts are there, two brothers, Greer and Blair. We spoke to them directly, and they both have an attitude I didn't like. They didn't allow us inside, but they claimed to have found the castle empty about four years ago. Said they had naught to do with killing the Muirs. Didn't realize it was Muir Castle, or so they claim."

Brodie Grant, Braden's sire, looked at him and said, "Something in your face tells me 'tis a lie. What does your sense say?"

Braden was not going to hold back. "I met Cairstine, daughter of the Muir. She said she was taken captive by the Lamonts several years ago."

"And did she confirm the Lamonts had killed her parents?" Uncle Alex asked, no expression at all on his face.

"Nay, not directly. We were interrupted when her son came out calling for her along with Greer Lamont. I was alone just outside the curtain wall, while she returned to the keep. I didn't get the chance to ask her everything I would have liked, but there's no doubt she is who she claims to be and does not wish to be held by the Lamonts. I promised her I would come back for her and take her away, but she's afraid the bastard will hunt her down and kill her and hurt her son if she left."

Uncle Alex sighed. "She's married to one of the brothers, then?"

"Nay, she says 'tis not so. She was taken captive, and, well, you can guess the rest. She was probably raped by the bastards, one or both of them, and now she stays on because of her son."

Uncle Alex paused to consider this while Roddy added, "We counted about fifty guards around the property. Not many. It would be easy to overtake them."

"We should slaughter them the same way they did the Muirs," Braden suggested, cracking his knuckles. He savored the thought. "But I also worry about the lad. We'd have to get inside to protect the two of them before forging an attack. But there's more that Cairstine led on to."

Roddy and Connor both gave quick nods at this revelation, and Braden had everyone's attention. "She said Lamont threatened that if she ran away again, he'd try to sell her son across the water."

Uncle Robbie repeated Braden's words, rubbing his hands together. "Across the water. Hellfire, but I hate bastards who take their anger out on bairns. Do you suppose that could mean they have a connection to the Channel of Dubh?"

Brodie said, "Or they know of it. Either way, I think we need to find out. Killing them is not the answer yet. We need more information. Much as I'd like to slaughter the bastards, that act would be counterproductive. They're supporting themselves in some elusive undertaking, if they've not made use of the land at all. It is certainly possible they could be part of the Channel of Dubh."

"Until we know for certain they were responsible for the Muirs' deaths, we'll not do any slaughtering. It seems likely, aye, but we've no solid evidence." Uncle Alex leaned back in his chair and stroked his chin. The man always gave careful consideration to every option before making a decision. While he was still the clan's chieftain, he'd given over many of his responsibilities to his two eldest lads, Jake and Jamie, after he suffered a wound in battle. The two were still on another mission or else would have been right at their sire's side.

"How are we going to determine that? If there were any witnesses left beyond the lass, we would have heard already," Uncle Robbie said.

Uncle Alex said, "Braden will have to get inside to speak with Muir's daughter again. If she's willing to claim the Lamont brothers killed her family and her sire's men, I'll have no trouble explaining to our king why we took action against the bastards. But she needs to have witnessed their actual deaths, not just assumed. Now, I'm sure these Lamonts are on high alert and will be for a few more days. Braden, you can make your move after that. I'm going to send a missive to Logan Ramsay, requesting Maggie and Will's expertise. I'd like them involved if this ambush could lead to any information about the Channel of Dubh. If you determine you need extra help, they'll be certain to assist you. They've broken out of the royal castle, and if they can get past the king's protective forces, they can certainly get past the Lamonts."

"That may be the best idea, Alex," his father said. "Braden struggles to control his anger when there's been a miscarriage of justice."

"I can if I need to, Papa," Braden retorted. "I'm not a bairn anymore." He had the sudden urge to bolt out of his chair and pace, but surely that wouldn't convince them of his self-control. "You'll never believe that I've conquered that fault, will you?"

His sire tilted his head. "I will when I've seen evidence of it. I've yet to." His words were harsh, but his tone was less so. "We can't afford to take any chances, is all. The fate of an innocent woman and child—and possibly many children—rests on the success of this mission."

Connor said, "He was extremely calm when he told us about what he'd learned on the journey back. I kept waiting for him to break out in his usual rant, but I never saw it."

Roddy added, "Me, either. Why is that, Braden?" he added with a smirk.

"I've told you. This is different. She's different. I'll not walk away from her or the promise I made."

Uncle Alex quirked his brow at Braden.

"I promised to get her and her son away from the Lamonts," he explained, leaning back in his chair with his hands folded on his lap. "She was too frightened to leave with me, but I will go back. You can count on it."

"I'll send that missive to Logan," Uncle Alex said. "Ask him what Maggie and Will are doing. I would like to wait a couple of days, catch the Lamonts off guard. If they arrive before then, they'll accompany you all. For now, I'd like to speak with Braden privately."

Braden waited to see if his sire would object, but he didn't. The four stood and left the solar without question. What had he done now?

Once the door closed, Braden waited for his uncle to speak. He had so much respect for Uncle Alex that he would wait patiently, even if it nearly killed him.

"I wanted to ask you about something that's been brought to my attention by several of your clanmates." His gaze stayed on Braden, that piercing look that could have made him pish down his leg when he was younger. Uncle Alex's expression could be intimidating enough to make you fear he was furious about something, but Braden couldn't recall ever seeing his uncle lose control. No doubt it would be a fearsome sight. The man was as large as a tree. In fact, he used to pretend he was a tree in the loch for Braden and his cousins, holding his arms out and swaying them so the lads crashed and fell into the water in fits of giggles. But Uncle Alex had never yelled, even when all the cousins had begun to bicker over who had hung on the longest.

Braden swallowed and waited.

"It's about Ronan. I know this is a painful subject, and I know you and Ronan have been loyal to each other since you were lads, but I need to be sure of something. Did you have an argument with Ronan the day before he died?"

If a faint breeze had passed him from the uncovered window, he'd have fallen off his chair. "An argument? With Ronan? Nay." He thought for a moment, trying to recall every event that had happened before his friend's death. Nothing came to mind.

Suddenly, he recalled a small battle they'd had in the lists. "We had a tussle, but it had been at least a sennight before his death. It wasn't an argument, just…" His memory filled in the pieces as he gave it more consideration. Ronan had taunted him about Roddy being a better swordsman than Braden. At first, they'd both laughed about it, but Ronan hadn't relented. Braden had allowed his temper to affect him, suddenly swinging his sword in a manner that revealed his mood and proved his point.

Ronan's response had been to drop his own weapon. That was what had brought attention to their wee tussle.

Ronan had said, "Teasing, Grant. Just trying to push you to be your best, but instead you let your temper in. You'll never keep your head with all that rage coursing through you. When will you learn to control your moods enough to hide them from your enemy? Someday you'll regret it."

Braden hadn't taken that comment well, instead moving over to grab him by his tunic. "I don't like your teasing. You worry about you, and I'll worry about me." Then he'd stalked off the practice field. His friend had called after him, "Control it, Grant."

Braden hung his head. True, he'd learned to control his temper around strangers or his elders, but could he do it in the heat of the moment? He had nearly forgotten the incident—it wasn't unusual enough to have made an impression, probably because it hadn't been unusual for him to lose his temper.

He needed to change that.

Uncle Alex asked, "Something come to mind? More than one person saw the two of you in the lists."

Braden reluctantly admitted, "We did argue about his habit of teasing me, and I didn't react well. But it was just healthy competitive banter between friends, Uncle, nothing more. And it was not the day before, but more than a sennight before."

"Did you threaten to kill him?"

"Nay!" he cried out in shock. "Kill my friend over something as immaterial as that? Never. Who told you…"

Uncle Alex held his hand up to indicate he wasn't going to share names. "You know I'll not reveal that, but one lad said you made a threat. I honestly couldn't believe you would do something like that. I've observed you often, Braden, but while you don't control your temper verra well, you've never intentionally hurt anyone to my knowledge. I don't believe you could have done aught to Ronan."

Braden whispered, "I did not push him over the cliff, Uncle Alex. I swear. I never would have hurt him. If anything, I would have jumped down to save him with half a thought to my own self." How he prayed his uncle believed him. The thought that anyone in his clan could believe him to be that shallow, that criminal, caused his palms to break out in sweat and his heartbeat to speed up.

Braden stared at the floor for a few moments, wondering if he could summon the courage to ask his uncle a question.

As if reading his mind, Uncle Alex asked, "What is it you wish to ask me? I'll answer if I can."

Braden thought for a moment, then said, "How do you do it? I've heard tales of your battle with the men who mistreated Aunt Maddie. You had a temper when you were younger, but I've never seen evidence of it. What do you do to keep it under control? I try, but 'tis still a struggle."

"When you allow your emotions into any battle, you'll harm your chance of winning. I learned that from a wise man, your grandfather, who you were not fortunate enough to know." He smiled and stared at a tapestry on the wall. "My sire had a wicked temper, and he paid a steep price because of it. One day in battle, he heard someone taunting him and took his eyes off his opponent, searching out the person who'd dared to speak to him so disrespectfully. He took a blade to his sword arm that rendered it useless for the rest of his days. He was past forty summers when it happened, so he didn't need to use it often, but he learned a powerful lesson that day. That the only man who stood in his way was himself.

"Every day after that, my sire said the same thing to me and my brothers each night. 'Control your temper or it will control you someday.'"

Uncle Alex was quiet for a long moment, allowing Braden the time to consider his words.

"Actually, 'twas your aunt Maddie who finally taught me to control my temper. I had a similar problem. Your sire and especially Uncle Robbie knew how to taunt me in the lists." He leaned back in his chair, a small smile curling his lips. "Aunt Maddie jumped every time I yelled. I wanted to court the lass, but my temper scared her away. That was when I finally learned to curtail my anger. Mayhap this lass will affect you the same."

Braden thought about that for a moment then said, "I can't imagine you yelling enough to frighten Aunt Maddie away."

"Ask her sometime. You're a good lad, nephew, but I see my sire's temper in you, and my own. Fight for the lass, but never fight for the sake of fighting. Purpose will see you through."

"You will help me fight for her, Uncle Alex?" He held his breath as he awaited an answer.

"Aye, we'll get her and her son away from the Lamonts. I'm tempted to send you back today and not subject her to another second of brutality, but we would do much better to wait and take them when they least expect it. They aren't leaving as I'm sure they've no place to go, and especially not if Muir Castle is a stronghold for the Channel of Dubh. The lass has survived her plight for nearly six years. Another sennight will not affect the ending."

A bundle of relief took over. "Many thanks, Uncle." He couldn't argue with his uncle's reasoning. Cairstine and her lad had survived, a testament to their strength. It made sense to wait if it improved their chances of success.

"You have an unusual interest in the lass, do you not?" Uncle Alex asked.

Braden didn't try to contain his surprise. "I suppose. Something about her is different. How could you tell?"

"I've seen that same look in my son's eyes. This is not just about righting a wrong for you. Still, the lass has been wronged without a doubt, and I won't do aught to try to stop you from becoming her champion. She deserves someone like you."

Braden whispered, "My thanks, Uncle Alex. I would like

to get to know her better, but I also fear I'll never see her again."

CHAPTER EIGHT

CAIRSTINE OPENED HER EYES, BUT the plethora of tears she'd shed overnight must have been enough to cause them to stick together. When she sat up, she searched the chamber for water, surprised to see a jug of it on a small table near the door. There was a chunk of bread and a goblet of mead next to it, too. Since she hadn't eaten anything since yesterday morn, she devoured the dark bread in three bites, washing it down with the mead.

She rinsed her mouth with the water from the jug, just then noticing the linen square resting beside it. She scrubbed her face, finishing with a sigh just as the sound of running feet reached her ears.

"Mama!" The rusty latch jostled, probably from Steenie doing his best to open it. She moved over to the window and peered down at him.

"Steenie, Mama's fine. Do not worry yourself." She arched her back, trying to get the aches out from sleeping on a wooden pallet with only one plaid on it.

"But Hilda said I could visit you. Corc promised he'd keep his eye on you, too," he added in a whisper. "Don't tell anyone." His sad eyes nearly broke her heart, but she didn't have much time to think on it since Hilda sauntered down the passageway, her keys jingling.

"Hilda. Please allow me inside," he said. "I miss my mama." Steenie kept his hand on the door handle all the while.

Hilda was the only nursemaid or healer the Lamonts had in their keep. She'd helped Cairstine throughout her pregnancy and birth, and without her, Cairstine wasn't at all sure she would have managed to get her son latched on to her breast. At six and ten, she'd known nothing about caring for a bairn. The nursemaid had also tended Steenie's sore bottom many times, though now that he was older, he was able to tolerate his punishment better.

Like Cairstine and Steenie, Hilda was not here by choice. The brothers had stolen her away from her home, but she didn't talk much about her life before. She did as she was told for fear of repercussions, but she'd always shown everyone kindness.

Hilda's ample bosom bounced as she made her way toward them. She'd never moved quickly, but she always went wherever she was needed. Her hands pushed the gray strands back into her plait where she could, her calculating gaze checking the interior of the chamber in one sweep. "Hush, lad. Hold your tongue. I'm not able to move at your pace." Before she put the key in the lock, she peeked through the window at Cairstine with a huge sigh. "What was it this time, lass?"

Cairstine blinked furiously to stop the tears that threatened to drench her cheeks. "What is it any time, Hilda?"

"Mama saw a man outside the curtain wall." He glanced over his shoulder before he continued. "She spoke with a Grant man they said. But I told them she did not do it apurpose. He tried to sneak in through the back wall. I told them you saved us from the man—that he might have killed us all if he got inside, but Papa doesn't believe me." His shoulders slumped as tears rolled down his cheeks. "Corc believes me though." That thought brought a hopeful look on his face.

God bless Corc and Hilda. Without their bread crusts of kindness, she and her son would starve.

"Steenie, Mama is just fine," she whispered at the same time Hilda jiggled the lock enough to open the door.

Hilda held the door while Steenie shoved past her and threw himself at Cairstine. Hilda said, "You have half an hour, then you must go, lad."

"You may stay and chat with us, Hilda," Cairstine offered. The woman's face changed to a look of sadness and she shook her head. "I have work to do. You know it falls on my shoulders, so I cannot stray for long." She shuffled back down the passageway, leaving Cairstine to wonder what assignment had taken away Hilda's natural smile.

She wasn't allowed to consider her quandary for long.

"Mama, why must you stay down here? How long must you stay?" He hadn't let go of her waist yet, still clinging to the one safe constant in his life.

"I'm not sure, but don't worry about me. Hilda brought me food and water. I'm sure Papa will allow me out later today."

Steenie's tears started anew, and he buried his face in her waist as his hitching sobs continued.

"Why do you cry, laddie?"

"Because I don't like it in the hall without you. Papa and Uncle Blair tease me always." He turned his head to the side once his sobs subsided, but he didn't let go of her waist.

She sat down and fussed with his hair, running her fingers through the strands in an effort to straighten them. "What was it this time, lad?"

"Papa says I'm not tall enough. He said I have to eat more, but I don't like that stew."

"If you don't like the stew, then eat more bread and cheese. You'll still grow to be big and strong, but you must eat."

"Why does Papa always yell at me so?" He sat on the pallet next to her and dropped his head onto her lap. The wistful expression on his face made her feel a stab of pity for both of them. "I know I'm supposed to love Papa, but sometimes I hate him, 'specially when he makes you stay down here."

"I don't have an answer." How she wished things were different. How she wished she could have gone with Braden Grant to live a different life, to find a world where men were honorable like the men in Clan Muir.

How would she know? Her sire had never treated her mother cruelly, but their relationship was one of the few she'd had occasion to observe. She had an aunt and uncle who'd lived in their own cottage inside the bailey. Even so, she'd never seen her uncle strike her aunt, or their two wee lassies. She had another aunt who lived alone, but she rarely saw her.

She had no idea what normal was any more. One of the most prominent memories she held of her family was how devoted her brother had always been to her sire. He'd never willingly left his side. As mean as Greer could be, he was still Steenie's sire, and Steenie adored him, though she was starting to see a change in the lad's attitude toward his sire.

Had he been paying attention when Braden Grant had said he didn't hit women? Had that left an impression on the lad? Steenie had been quick to point out on Drummond land that his sire hit him, also. Greer had been much tougher on the lad of late, and Steenie's love was being tested. Bairns unconditionally loved their parents, but this could turn into something entirely different.

How she struggled with this. Someday, Steenie would wonder where his grandparents were, and what would she tell him? That his own father had ordered and enacted the killing of all her brethren?

And yet another voice in her head encouraged her not to give up on escaping. It insisted she needed to save her sweet son before he became like the cruel man who'd destroyed her family. If that were to happen, it would be the thing to utterly destroy her. She wanted revenge desperately, but how was she to get it?

She hugged Steenie, rocking him back and forth like she'd done when he was a wee babe in her arms.

"Mama, I know what I'll do if Papa does not free you from here," he whispered.

"What?"

"I'll go find one of the Grants. They'll save you."

"Steenie, nay. If Papa caught you, he'd be verra angry."

"But I'm verra angry with Papa. What else can I do?"

"Naught. Do not risk another thrashing. Please? I'll not be with you to hold you when he's finished." How she wished she had an answer for her son. There was little any of them could do to fight the Lamont brothers.

A face appeared in the window. "Your time is up, lad." Corc stood in the open doorway with his hands on his hips. "Sorry you're stuck in here, lass. I've tried to convince him you've been locked away for long enough."

"Just a few more moments, Corc. I miss my mama." Steenie smiled as he stared up at her, comforted by her hand rubbing his back.

It was one of his favorite comforts, getting a back rub. Before he had hair, he'd loved having his head rubbed.

"You'll watch over him for me, Corc?" she asked.

"Aye. 'Tis why I'm here. I asked Greer if I could have him out at the stables. Said I needed help mucking the stalls. He's a hard worker." Steenie didn't make a comment, so he added, "I can keep an eye on him during the day for you, at least until you're released from here."

"Thank you."

God bless Corc.

———◆———

BRADEN STEPPED INSIDE THE GRANT great hall, overflowing with clanmates attracted by the delicious aromas wafting from the overflowing festival tables. Aunt

Maddie planned several festivals during the year, but one of the favorites was always the early summer festival. Anxious to get outside in the fresh air, everyone came out of the cottages to join with the laird's family in the great hall and the courtyard, if the weather accommodated them. Braden enjoyed their clan festivals, chatting with his numerous cousins about memories and sharing stories about their many Ramsay cousins, but he knew tonight he'd be preoccupied.

Preoccupied with the memory of a lass with green eyes in his arms. But there was nothing he could do until his uncle gave him permission to leave with a group of warriors, so he forced his mind elsewhere.

Aunt Maddie, Uncle Alex's wife, stood near the doorway. "Braden, 'tis lovely to see you again. I have your favorite pork meat pies ready for you."

He greeted her with a hug. "Many thanks to you, Aunt Maddie. I will enjoy them. And I might try a pastry or two, if you don't mind." He thought of his conversation with his uncle earlier. "Aunt Maddie, may I ask you a question?"

"Of course, Braden. What is it?"

"Did Uncle Alex used to have a temper and yell verra often?"

She chuckled. "He most certainly did. Before we were married, he used to yell loud enough to be heard in England. 'Twas a long time ago, Braden. He's changed since then."

Roddy came up behind them, pulling them both into his embrace for a moment. "Do I smell meat pies, Aunt Maddie?"

"Aye," she said with a laugh, "and I have a few mutton pies for you, Roddy. Pardon me, lads, but I must assist Cook in the kitchens."

She disappeared into the kitchens, and he and Roddy shifted their attention to the array of pies.

Roddy said with a wry grin, "I'll let you go first, cousin.

Just in case you wish to peruse the varieties, choose the best one." He held his hands up in a mock gesture. "I promise not to get in your way."

Connor joined them. "Is Braden keeping you from the meat pies, Roddy?"

Braden snorted. "Funny. You're both making me laugh. But as long as you both insist, I'll grab mine first." He reached for a pork pastry, elbowing Roddy along the way.

They made their way through the crowded hall, checking out the other fare. "Hellfire, I love these pork pies," Braden gave a short moan after he bit into one plump pie filled with pork and carrots covered in a rich gravy.

Connor asked, "You have not eaten lately, Braden? You seem a bit hungry."

"You are not?" Roddy asked, stuffing the rest of his first pie into his mouth.

"I'm hungry, but for a pair of sweet lips to taste, not meat pies." His gaze searched the hall, surveying all the young lasses in attendance. "The early summer festival usually has the most lassies only because 'tis not too cold outside. I'm hoping to find one who's willing to take a stroll into the night a wee bit later. Mayhap steal a kiss or two."

The oddest thing happened. As soon as Connor mentioned lasses, all Braden could think of was the golden-haired lass who had trembled in his arms and then run away from him. Though he tried to focus on other things, he couldn't.

Cairstine Muir had left an impression on him, just as Uncle Alex had guessed. His gaze traveled around the hall, and it surprised him not one bit that he found no one who could compare to her. They all appeared young and immature, the opposite of Cairstine, who'd been forced to mature at a very young age.

He longed to touch her soft skin, to run his hands down her soft hips and breasts. Not many young lasses had the hips he preferred. He wanted a lass who would match his passion, move with him, fit him just right. He'd noticed while she had sweet curves in the right places, she was thin. Did the bastards starve her, too? He did his best not to think about all that Cairstine and her son had to deal with in the Lamont holding.

Cairstine was all woman, though she could be no more than twenty summers. He had just turned ten and nine, so it was entirely possible that she was a wee bit older than him.

As he was lost in his reverie, a cute lass with long dark waves sidled up to the three of them, sashaying her hips just so. "Good eve, lads. Is that all you plan on doing, eating meat pies? I can think of other things I'd prefer to do. I have a friend who I could bring along."

Connor noticed his sire coming so he said, "I'd love to take a stroll with you later, Lora. Anyone else interested?" He turned to his cousins.

"I'll join you," Roddy said, glancing at Braden.

Braden shook his head, not wishing to hurt her feelings, but only interested in taking a stroll with one lass in particular. And he wouldn't be satisfied until he had her back in his arms.

"Meet us near the door in half an hour."

Lora nodded with a sweet curve of her lips, then whirled around to head in the opposite direction.

Connor said, his gaze following the sway of her hips, "She's bonny, is she not?"

"She's all yours, Connor," Braden said. These local girls did little to turn his head, especially these days. He had always felt the need to wait for a lass who would challenge him, and Cairstine was definitely that.

Uncle Alex strolled across the hall, heading directly toward the tables laden with food—meat pies, fresh bread, a multitude of cheeses, as well as small trenchers that could be filled with lamb stew.

Uncle Alex greeted the three of them before patting

Braden on the shoulder and heading for the kitchens. Moments later, he reappeared with a giant trencher, which he loaded with stew until it nearly overflowed.

Roddy whispered, "'Tis the way to do it. Aunt Maddie must make special ones for Uncle Alex. Look at the size of it."

Braden said, "Never mind that. May I ask you two a question in private?"

Both cousins merely nodded, mostly because their mouths were still full of food. Braden ushered them away from the table so they wouldn't be overheard. He wasn't quite sure how to start the conversation but decided that being direct would work best. If he couldn't trust his cousins to answer honestly, who else could he ask?

"Do you think my temper has become better or worse of late?"

Roddy spat his food into his hand, and Connor choked on whatever he'd had in his mouth, coughing as his gaze caught Braden's. Roddy tossed his food into a pail meant for garbage before returning to them. "Are you serious, cousin?"

Connor grinned, his eyes dancing with delight.

"Aye, I'm serious. I know I have lost my temper a few times in the past, but it doesn't happen verra often any more. Do you not agree?"

Connor said, "You've always had a hot temper. Do you not recall when your sire threw you in the snowbank?"

"What?" Braden asked, unable to recall the incident Connor mentioned. "I don't recall aught about a snowbank." He scowled as he searched for any memory of the event.

"You don't remember?" Connor asked in disbelief. "You and Roddy were upset with Kyla and Gracie for taking something of yours. Kyla gave it back, but you kept yelling and yelling."

Roddy burst into gales of laughter. "I remember now.

And you wanted Kyla to get a thrashing. Kept shouting at Uncle Alex."

"Stomped your foot a few times, too. You were madder than a slobbering, stiff-legged boar before a battle. How old were you, Roddy?"

"I don't remember how old I was, but I remember it well. He was stalking and stomping. I'll never forget it. I knew he was going to get into trouble, so I didn't veer far away."

"You enjoyed watching me get into trouble?"

Both cousins nodded, wicked smirks on their face. Roddy said, "Back then? Of course, I was just glad 'twasn't me."

Braden's mind started to pull bits and pieces of the memory back. In fact, had he spat at something?

Connor started to laugh again, the kind that was contagious, the kind he couldn't control. He managed to get a few words out, "In fact, you were so mad at Kyla that you ran across the entire length of the hall, came to an abrupt stop in front of the hearth, and you spat in it loud enough that Aunt Maddie came running down the stairs because she thought someone was heaving, and…and…" Guffaws erupted straight from his belly. "Then you turned around and headed straight for Kyla again, screaming at her. You called her a bitch."

Roddy finished the story. "Uncle Alex nodded to your sire, and your sire picked you up under his arm and tossed you outside…" He looked at Connor and started laughing. "And you cussed your sire out. I could hear you wailing as you went out the door."

Connor took up the tale. "And I peeked out past your sire. He threw you into a snowbank off to the side and spun around, but you kept yelling." Connor swiped at the tears in his eyes. "You started shivering and said, 'Papa, Kyla stole my sword. You have to thrash her. She's a witch.' Then you had to stop because you were shivering so much. I would have shut my mouth at that point, but you kept hollering at your sire."Your father said…" He bent over at the waist laughing, and then stood up again. "'If you don't stop your bellowing, I'll throw you in the loch next.'"

Roddy said,"And you still argued, so your sire ran toward you and you took off toward the gates. He finally stopped and told you not to come back until you could stop your complaining."

Connor said,"I laughed so hard I nearly pished myself. I was truly hoping he'd throw you in the loch. Of course, your mother wanted to go after you, but your sire wouldn't allow it."

Braden stared at his two cousins doubled over in hysterical laughter. They were starting to draw a crowd. He remembered landing in the snowbank, shocked that his own sire would do such a thing. As soon as he'd gone back inside, he'd burst into tears, but not before throwing ten snowballs at the stones in the keep walls. When a couple of tears froze to his face, he stopped weeping.

Mayhap he did have a wee bit more of a temper than he'd thought. It seemed to be a quality that dated far back in his childhood. Perhaps he was even born with it.

Connor took two deep breaths and stopped laughing. "Ten minutes later, you opened the door shivering. You apologized for your behavior and asked permission to come inside. When your sire nodded, you ran over to the hearth to warm up."

"Shite," he whispered, the only thing he could think of to say at the moment."I barely remember it, but I do recall freezing in the snowbank and throwing ten snowballs at the keep."

"'Twas funny," Roddy said. "Sorry to laugh, but you were young. You haven't behaved that poorly in a while. Now you might throw five instead of ten snowballs. I'd say you've properly matured."

While his cousins struggled to contain their laughter, he

said, "But my point was that I've improved my self-control over the years. I've learned to be less impulsive. Do you not agree?"

Before either one could answer, Uncle Alex came over, still chewing on pieces of his trencher. "What's causing all this laughter?"

Connor said, "We were just teasing Braden. Remember the time Uncle Brodie threw him in the snowbank?"

Uncle Alex turned to Braden. He didn't laugh like Roddy and Connor did, but there was a spark of merriment in his eyes. "Aye, I do recall, but you got over it, lad. Remember that."

His uncle's words filled him with hope because if he knew one thing, it was that he had to learn how to keep himself under control. Otherwise, he could end up just like Greer Lamont, and he would never want to put Cairstine through that again.

He would do whatever it took to be a good man for her.

CHAPTER NINE

———◆———

S TEENIE STARED UP AT THE beams over the great
hall. He had a pallet in the corner just like many of the
guards did, but he hated it.

He wanted his mother. Rolling onto his side, he peeked
over the group to see if anyone else was awake. This was
the usual time he'd sneak up to his mother's chamber and
climb into bed with her. She was softer and warmer than
the stupid pallet he slept on. And she never turned him
away.

He loved his papa, but sometimes he hated him, too.
How could he be so mean to his mama? She smelled nice
and took care of him and loved him. Besides, she never
yelled at him the way his sire did. Papa yelled even when
Steenie didn't do aught wrong.

At least Corc had spent time with him yesterday. They'd
had fun cleaning out a stall and then a horse had pooped
right in front of them. It smelled so bad that Corc had
coughed and turned all green and Steenie thought he was
going to heave. Steenie laughed so hard he couldn't hold
in his own gas. Mama would have been upset with him,
but Corc thought it was funny.

He stayed with him all day, until Corc sent him to the
keep for the night, though he would rather have slept in
the hay next to the horses.

He thought of the Grant warriors he'd seen, how strong

they looked. The one with the black hair looked the biggest of them all. He was strong just like the one they saw on Drummond land, though that one was shorter. His arms were as big as tree trunks like the yellow-haired warrior, but the odd thing was that in spite of his size, he hadn't seemed mean at all, not like his sire and Uncle Blair could be.

He had to help his mama out of that cold place in the cellars. But he didn't know what to do. He'd asked his sire to set her free, but Papa had just swatted his bottom and told him to be quiet.

No one was awake and he had to pish, so he rolled off his pallet, grabbed the wooden sword his papa had given him, sheathed it, and crept outside to do his business. No one spoke to him on his way out. He strolled through the courtyard until he made it to the stables, then hid behind the back and pished, making sure no one was watching him. He didn't want any more thrashings for a while because his bottom was just starting to get better. If only he could figure out how to be better so his thrashings would stop. His mother always told him to be good, but he always was. There was naught he could do to make his sire happy.

When he finished, he moved back toward the center of the courtyard, but he caught something out of the corner of his eye. He pulled his sword out as fast as the Grant warriors had, holding it in front of him in case it was some wild animal about to attack, but he didn't see anything.

He liked swinging his sword, so he practiced unsheathing it a few more times until he could do it faster. That would surely make Papa proud. Before he knew it, he had ambled down past the stables. He wondered if he could use the sword atop a horse, so he crept back to the stables, surprised to see Corc and the others were all sleeping. He couldn't saddle the horse by himself so he went back to the gates and practiced some more. He'd be the fastest and strongest of all warriors someday.

As his dance became more fluid, he decided he needed to practice his war whoop. He moved away from the gates because he didn't wish to wake the guards asleep at the gates. The clearing called to him, so he raced over there and whipped his sword out before he growled and ran toward a tree with his sword over his head.

He searched for a fallen log and finally found one where he could swing his sword over his hand and connect with the soft wood. It hadn't been very long when he found another log and then another. He'd be the best ever by the time he finished practicing.

When his arms tired out, he stopped for a moment and searched around to see where he was, only to find a small problem. He had no idea. Staring up at the moon, he sheathed his sword and began to count the number of stars he could see. His mama had taught him to count to fifty.

When he couldn't find any more, he tipped his head back as far as he could and giggled because he got dizzy. He tried it again but thought he saw something. Spinning around with his sword drawn, his fear turned to delight when he saw a brown pony standing in front of him. Once he sheathed his sword, the animal nudged his hand with his cold nose. Steenie laughed and moved over to wrap his arms around his neck with a giggle.

"What's your name, pony?"

The beast snorted at him, tipping his head up and shaking it, his white mane bouncing.

"You want me to give you a name?" He thought for a moment, chewing on his lip. "Hmmm. I like the name Padraig. 'Tis it! I'll call you Paddy the Pony."

The pony rubbed against him, so he decided to climb up and see where he would take him. Since his sire was sleeping, he was quite sure he could ride for a wee bit without getting caught. Then he'd return to the keep right away.

Paddy was a new friend, something he needed. He'd always wished for a friend.

"Paddy, you can be my friend forever. Do you like me? I like you. I don't have any friends. Corc told me someday I would. He knew you'd come to me, did he not?" He patted his neck as he situated himself on Paddy's back, surprised he came with his saddle already on, ready to go.

He grabbed the reins and aimed him back toward the direction he thought the keep was in, but Paddy headed in the opposite direction, trotting at a pretty good pace until they were deep in the forest.

He tried his best to stop him and turn him around, but the wee animal had a mind of his own. "Paddy, you're going the wrong way. Papa will thrash me again if I don't go back. Turn around, Paddy." He pulled on the reins again, but the wee beast ignored him, continuing on his own route.

"Paddy, you cannot be my friend if you make me get a thrashing. Bad pony," he said, doing his best to scold the small horse, but Paddy's only response was to shake his head and snort on occasion.

Since he couldn't change their direction, Steenie decided he'd practice his skills to make his sire proud. He'd be so proud of him that he'd surely forget to thrash him. He sheathed and unsheathed his sword over and over again until he got really good at it. When he thought he couldn't do it any better, he stopped the pony and turned around, only he had no idea where he was. This time he knew he was far away from his castle.

Frowning, he glanced up at the nearly full moon, glad it gave enough light to see his surroundings.

He'd kill anyone who threatened him, just like a grown-up warrior would do.

All of a sudden, he had a thought. He'd gotten this far without anyone seeing him, and if Papa caught him this far away from the keep, he'd get another thrashing for sure. He glanced around, saying a quick prayer that he wouldn't see his sire or his uncle nearby, but all was quiet in the meadow.

He made his mind up to do what his da often told him. He was about to act like a man.

He was going to find the Grants and save his mother. "Paddy," he said with authority, "take me to Clan Grant. We must find the man with the arms like tree trunks to help Mama."

———◆———

BRADEN LEFT HIS COUSINS ONCE he noticed Marta slip through the doorway of the great hall. Uncle Alex had informed him of the new tales that were being whispered about him and Ronan, but he had to know if Marta believed them, or if she thought their quick morning chat had caused the problem. He had to uncover exactly what others were thinking.

Marta jumped when he touched her elbow from the side. "Good eve to you, Marta. How do you fare?" He couldn't let go of the fact that Ronan had thought Marta was involved with someone else, but she had distinctly denied it. Somehow, he felt he owed it to his friend to uncover the truth.

He also wished to allay his own fears about the rumors. The event between the two of them the week before could not have affected Ronan that strongly. He was sure of it, but he hoped Marta would confirm it for him. Had Ronan been upset about their tussle, he would have told her.

She smiled, a nervous smile, but at least she was able to smile. "I am well, Braden. Time is healing my heart."

"I am glad to hear it. I know you've sworn that there had been no one else, but I'm still bothered by all the events that led up to that day. I need to ask you a question if you do not mind."

"What is it?"

"Did you see Ronan at all the day before he died? I

know we discussed this before, but have you thought of anything new?"

"Aye, I saw him, but only for a short time. He stopped at my home to chat, but 'twas after the lists, so he needed to clean up. But I already told you this."

"Would you mind answering again? I'm still bothered by what happened. I'm trying to make sense of it. Did he mention aught about any arguments?"

"Nay, why? Oh, I think I understand. You heard the talk about your argument with Ronan the week before in the lists, that you upset him too much, which may have been part of the reason for his...well...you know of what I speak." She stared at the ground, a rosy color blossoming across her cheeks, but then she lifted her chin. "Nay, he did not mention you. I've heard the other whispers, too, and I feel compelled to say again that I was not interested in any other lad. I spoke to no one except in passing. I saw you that morn and one other. 'Twas naught more than polite chatting on both occasions."

Braden sighed with relief. He hadn't truly believed he'd upset Ronan, but he was glad to hear Marta validate his thoughts. "Would you like to sit and chat a bit?"

"Nay. My thanks for your consideration, Braden, but I think it best if I'm not associated with you for a while. I hope you understand." She gave him a strained smile and walked away.

He wasn't quite sure whether he should be offended or not. But now another question niggled at him.

If Ronan hadn't taken his own life because Marta was interested in another man, what had forced him to take such a drastic measure?

———◆———

CAIRSTINE WAS JARRED AWAKE BY a noise farther down the passageway, a haunting noise...almost like a crying bairn. Nay, more than one bairn—there were many.

She closed her eyes again because she knew it had to be a dream. There were no bairns in the keep. There used to be, many years ago when it was the Muir keep, but no more. There were very few lasses here, only Hilda and Cairstine and those who lived in the kitchens.

Only she did *not* fall back to sleep and the sobs persisted. She sat up on her pallet, tipping her head as if that could make the sounds clearer.

Standing, she moved over to the door and put her ear to the window, listening carefully for the soft cries to begin again. She was about ready to give up when she heard them. No mistaking it. They were the distant cries of bairns who could be anywhere from five to twelve summers old. The haunting sounds echoed down the eerie passageway, evidence of unhappiness that was greater than her own somewhere in the dark cellars.

She had no idea what to do, except she could do nothing, could she? She was in a locked chamber. Lying down on her pallet again, she allowed herself to fall into a fitful sleep, full of eerie dreams.

The next time she awakened, she heard the jingling of the keys outside the door. Could it be Steenie and Hilda? Moments later, it banged open and Greer barged in, a look of uncontrolled fury on his face that made her cringe back toward the cold wall.

"Where's Steenie?" His voice had that threatening tone she dreaded.

Her mind raced to the worst possible conclusion. Was he hurt? Missing? "I don't know. I've not seen him since yester morn. He's not in his bed?"

"He's not been seen since he climbed into his pallet last eve. Did he tell you he was running away?"

"Nay, Greer. I swear. He wants me out of here, but he said naught about leaving. Did you check with Corc? Mayhap he went to visit him. Or mayhap he's stuck in a chamber down the passageway. I heard bairns crying in the middle of the night."

In the quietest voice she'd ever heard from the *bastart*, he asked, "You heard what?"

"Bairns crying. We must go investigate. Mayhap Steenie came searching for me in his sleep and got lost. The sound might have echoed down here."

"You'll never mention that again." He grabbed ahold of her arm and tugged her close.

"Mention what? Steenie missing? Please, Greer, you're hurting me."

"Do you hear me? You heard naught last night, and you'll never repeat what you just said. Whatever you heard, 'twas not Steenie." A small tic in his eye started, something she recognized as a sign of a temper.

Still, she couldn't stop herself. "We have to go investigate! I'll go with you. If it wasn't Steenie, there may still be other bairns down here. I'm sure it wasn't a dream."

"Did you not hear me? I said you're not to speak of it again, nor will we consider such a ridiculous claim." He flung her across the chamber. She tried to catch her fall but tripped over the pallet and stumbled onto the ankle that had already been weakened.

She couldn't stop her head from slamming against the stone wall. The last thing she saw before she crumpled to the ground was Greer reaching for her, but he was too late.

Cairstine saw stars before the rest of the world went black.

CHAPTER TEN

STEENIE RODE HIS PONY THROUGH the valley, wondering if he was headed in the right direction. As soon as the sun came up, he'd thought they were heading north, and he'd heard the Grant leader say they lived south of his family's castle. But he didn't really know for sure because he was confused. "Paddy, I hope you know how to get to Grant land. If not, we could be in big trouble."

Paddy was two-toned with brown fur and speckles of white that matched his mane. He was quite handsome, but Steenie could tell he was tiring. The sun was nearly up so they'd traveled farther than he thought. He brought him over to a stream, and he drank loudly and heavily.

"Paddy, I'm sorry if you're working too hard, but you must get me far enough away so my sire won't find me." His hands went to protect his bottom. "You know how he likes to thrash me, and I cannot ride when he does. 'Tis barely tolerable now, but I must do this for my mama." He dismounted, washed his hands, and took a drink before moving back to Paddy. Before he climbed on Paddy's back, he stopped in front of him and said, "I'm getting hungry, too. How much longer to Grant land?" He stared into the animal's eyes, but he couldn't tell anything at all from him. "I wish you could talk to me and be a real friend."

The horse knickered and nudged him, startling him into a fit of giggles. "I love you, Paddy." He petted his mane and mounted, leading him away from the stream.

They hadn't traveled far when he heard a group of horses headed his way. He located a group of trees and did his best to hide, going deeper into the dense forest than he would have normally dared. He dismounted so he could go farther still, whispering to Paddy, "You must be quiet for a wee bit. I'll come back for you. Please don't leave me." Then he hurried until he found his own large tree trunk to hide behind while Paddy grazed.

"Hold!" he heard a voice bellow. The approaching horses came to a stop. He'd guessed there were less than a dozen beasts, but that meant a dozen men. Tears flowed down his cheeks because he knew if it was his sire, he was in for a beating for certes.

The other possibilities weren't much better. It could be a group of reivers or his uncle Blair or maybe even the king's men! They'd bring him home for certain and then he'd take a beating and still not have finished his mission.

And what would happen to his new friend?

He tried to stop his tears by pinching his eyes closed, but it did not work. His nose was running, but if he sniffled they'd hear him for sure. The rustle of leaves and the crack of twigs told him they were not far. It sounded like two men had taken up the search.

They came closer.

And closer.

And he nearly pished himself as they approached the other side of the tree he hid behind. He was too scared to look around the trunk.

A moment later, a young voice called to him. "You can come out. We won't hurt you." It sounded like a lad, so he hesitantly peeked out from behind the tree. A man in a Grant plaid stared at him and a big lad, wearing the same plaid, nodded. "We'll not hurt you. What's your name?"

"Steenie," he said, fearful of what would happen next. Would they take him prisoner, tie him up like his sire often did with strangers? Would they beat him? He tried not to cry at his thoughts, but it was hard. He whispered, "Who are you?"

"I'm Kenzie. This is my sire."

The tall man said, "My name is Loki Grant, and we're here to help you, lad. Do not fear us."

———————

BRADEN AND RODDY BROKE THEIR fast with their fathers, plus Alex and Connor, before dawn the next morn, ahead of the usual group. Uncle Alex had requested they all meet early to make plans.

Braden waited as patiently as possible, glancing at Roddy to see if he would say anything to help the situation along.

Uncle Alex was the first to speak. "I'd like to send about fifty guards to the Lamont property on the morrow. You three will lead the group, so choose your warriors."

"With what intent?" Connor asked.

Braden couldn't restrain his natural impulse. "Kill the bastards."

Uncle Alex quirked his brow at Braden, who quickly closed his mouth. His uncle said, "Braden, you know we cannot go in and slaughter them without good reason unless you'd enjoy seeing my head on a pike."

"Why not? They slaughtered the Muirs, an entire clan innocent."

"'Tis as I've said. We need a witness and we have none. Suppose we kill both brothers and then discover that only one of them was involved with murdering the Muirs. They've caused no trouble that I'm aware of since then. What charges have we?"

"But they must have done it! Muir's daughter will testify."

"Until the daughter informs you of their guilt directly, you're to do nothing unless you are defending yourselves. I would also like for you to go to the nearest cottages to the west of them, see if you can uncover aught else about them. Mayhap some of their neighbors have heard or seen bairns. Before we blindly start killing men, I need more proof. Not to mention, we need them alive to answer questions about their potential involvement in the Channel of Dubh."

Braden's sire said, "If they are not involved in the Channel of Dubh, then one would wonder where they get their coin. That land is not fertile, and according to Roddy, there were no fields to be seen. What do they eat?"

Roddy said, "I'm sure they've reived a few cattle, mayhap sheep as well."

Connor said, "Mayhap they sell whisky."

Connor's sire pursed his lips. "I could mayhap consider the whisky if Muir had made his own liquid gold. Without a helping hand, they wouldn't be able produce much in a few years. They must be reiving, or they'd have naught to eat except what they killed. But thievery is undependable and will not feed a group alone. After what Braden told us about the threat Greer made to sell the lad over the water, mayhap they've become involved in something more. I sent the missive to the Ramsays. If Will and Maggie arrive shortly, I'll send them along. I want their opinion on this as you know they are in the king's favor."

"If I can find Cairstine and she tells us the Lamonts are both guilty, do we have your permission to attack?" Braden pressed.

The Grant brothers exchanged long looks. Braden's sire was the one who finally answered him. "That would depend on the number of guards they have. They'll know you're in the area, so you'll not take them by surprise. You would need over a hundred warriors to be safe. Should we send more, Alex?"

"Nay. Fifty should be plenty, but if you need more and have the grounds to attack, send a messenger and I'll release as many warriors as you need. If we send any more upfront, they'll feel threatened and attack first. Any other questions?"

"When do we leave?" Roddy asked.

"At dawn on the morrow," Uncle Alex said. "Give you time to choose the right warriors."

The others left, but Braden held back. "My apologizes, Uncle Alex, for interrupting you with my opinion. I am too impulsive." He gave his uncle a sheepish grin because that was all he had to offer. He'd lost his temper just a wee bit. Now that he'd begun to pay attention to his actions, he'd noticed he allowed his temper freer rein than he'd realized.

"You're forgiven, lad. At least you recognized it. You were able to control yourself better than you have in the past." He patted Braden on the shoulder and headed out of the hall. "Your thinking's getting sharper, more strategic. The sign of a true warrior is when a man can lead on solid judgement as opposed to heeding his impulses. You'll continue to learn. We all have ways we can improve."

Braden grabbed another hunk of bread and headed outside. He caught up with his cousins as they passed several guards heading in to break their fasts. Some ate at home, some came for the porridge Aunt Maddie made available for any warriors.

Connor asked, "Everything set for the morrow? There are no changes?"

"Nay," Braden said, lowering his voice. "I needed to apologize to your sire for momentarily losing my head."

Roddy and Connor glanced at each other before returning their gaze to Braden. "Well, well, well. Sounds like you *are* maturing. Apparently that little talk we had made you decide to avoid any more snowbanks in your future." Roddy jested. "Let's get down to business, though. How do you wish to choose our guards?"

They made a plan, then headed out to the lists. Some were already there, so Braden made the announcement about choosing warriors for the morning journey. As soon as they said there might be a battle, volunteers barraged them for a place on the team. While they practiced daily, they didn't see battle often, and the youngest of the group usually begged to be involved in any possible combat.

Braden joined Roddy, who stood talking with Moray and Keith.

Keith said, "You wish to spar with me? I'll take you on."

"Sure," Braden replied, unsheathing his sword and taking a couple of practice swings. "We'll see if you're strong enough to earn the right to travel with us on the morrow."

Keith grinned. "I plan to be there." He unsheathed his weapon and went at Braden with little warning, but he easily defended himself.

The two practiced for a while without any conversation, Roddy and Moray quietly observing them. After a short time, Braden decided to put a question to the brothers. The matter had been weighing on him. "You both well know that I've been trying to understand what drove Ronan to take his own life. I can't well wrap my head around it and until I do, I'm afraid I won't be at peace. I spoke with Marta at the festivities last eve, and she swears there was no one else in her life but Ronan. Did he truly believe she'd strayed?"

"He told Mama he believed there was someone else. Why can't you let this go and try to heal like the rest of us?" Keith asked, furrowing his brow.

"Because I want answers. I don't believe Ronan would take his own life, even with a good reason." Braden swung in a circle, bringing the flat of his sword against the hilt of Keith's sword, but he blocked it since both of them were familiar with that move.

"I don't know what to tell you, Grant, but 'tis what Mama said. I've never known my mother to lie."

"I would never call your mother a liar. Don't misconstrue my question." How else could he find the information he needed but to ask those closest to Ronan? His guilt over his failure to realize his friend was hurting had struck him.

"Mayhap you're trying to distract all the attention from you to another," Moray said from the sidelines.

The words had bite to them, and Braden shifted his position to get a better look at the man. Still, he had not forgotten Uncle Alex's advice. He did his best to focus on his opponent and not on another lad's words.

"What do you mean, Moray?" he asked carefully, trying not to provoke him.

"Mayhap 'tis your fault, but you can't accept that and you want to find another to blame."

Braden set his sword down and stepped back from Keith, wiping the sweat from his brow. "You have it wrong, Moray. I just want answers. Don't we all wish for the same?"

"Is it true, Braden? Did you upset my brother the day before he jumped?" Keith asked.

"Nay," Braden barked, though he fought his instincts and controlled his temper to the best of his ability. "Those words we had were long before he jumped."

"Then stop stirring up trouble," Moray bellowed. "We've been through enough." He whirled around and stalked off the field, drawing the attention of a few others in the lists. Thankfully, their attention was quickly diverted again by something Connor had announced to the crowd about what skills he wished to observe.

"Ignore him," Keith said. "He just wishes to stop talking about Ronan. He misses him."

Braden agreed, since the entire conversation had gained him naught. He grabbed a nearby skin of water and took several swigs—only to nearly drop it when he saw a new group of warriors at the stables. He recognized his adopted brother Loki and Loki's adopted son Kenzie.

But it was the lad who'd dropped from his horse and come running straight toward them who'd caught his attention.

Cairstine's son.

He motioned to Roddy and the two of them headed toward the newcomers, but the lad didn't slow. Once he reached them, he launched himself at Roddy, screaming, "Please save my mama."

The lad was upset and exhausted.

What's wrong with your mother, lad," Braden pressed, "and where is she?"

He looked at Braden and said, "My name is Steenie, and Papa put Mama in the cellars. He locked her up and won't let her out. I ran away to find someone to save her. Please help Mama."

Judging by the expressions on their faces, Loki and Roddy did not recognize the lad, but his words filled Braden with urgency. The arsehole had locked her up?

"We found him hiding in the trees alone, and he insisted that we bring him to the Grants, specifically you, Roddy," Loki explained. "He was looking for the yellow-haired Grant with arms like tree trunks."

Roddy glanced at his upper arms and then grinned. "You wanted me, lad? How do you know me?"

"I saw you when you came to my castle. My papa made me watch from the top of the curtain wall."

Loki looked at Braden. "He's pretty young to be out on his own. You have any idea who he's talking about?"

Braden managed a hasty nod. He was anxious for the lad to talk, but he forced himself to act calmly. Kneeling down next to the bairn, he said, "Steenie, your mama's name is Cairstine, is it not?"

"Aye, she shouldn't be locked up. My da did it." He could see the signs of the lad's exhaustion.

"Did you ride all night?"

He nodded his wee head, tears appearing in his eyes. "I went out to take a pish and I got distracted. My mama always tells me to pay 'tention to what I'm doing but I forgot where I was. I practiced my sword because I was mad. Then Paddy the Pony found me, and he carried me this way. I tried to make him go back, but he wouldn't, and then I wanted to save my mama and I thought I could find you before my da discovered me missing, because if he finds me…" His hands moved to his backside.

"Tell him who your da is," Loki instructed.

"Greer Lamont. I love my papa, but sometimes he's mean, especially to Mama. Papa wouldn't let her out. Will you help me?" He glanced from Roddy to Braden and then back to Loki. "Please? I brought my sword. I can help, though Papa will give me a thrashing if I swing it at him."

Braden patted his shoulder. "Do not fash. We'll help you, lad, you can count on it."

Loki whistled for Kenzie to join them. The lad was still standing near the stables, but he came charging over, his words already flying out of his mouth. "Will you help him, Uncle Braden? Papa and I will go with you."

Loki said, "We'll help him, Kenzie. Why don't you take Steenie to the hall and get him something to eat? Are you hungry, lad?"

Steenie nodded. "Will you take care of Paddy? Please don't let him leave. He's my new pet. He's hungry, too."

Kenzie said, "I already fed your pony. We can go eat, I think Paddy's tired."

"All warriors must eat," Loki said, motioning for Kenzie to take Steenie to the hall. The two made a wild dash toward the keep.

Loki said, "You know the situation, Braden?"

"Aye, I do, and you can count on me getting the bairn's mother out of the cellars."

"How do you plan to do that?"

Braden managed to lower his voice, barely, though he seethed on the inside.

"If I have to, I'll kill Greer Lamont."

CHAPTER ELEVEN

CAIRSTINE OPENED HER EYES, THEN promptly shut them. A persistent throbbing on one side of her head claimed her attention. She reached up to hold her head, hoping to calm the pounding, but her fingers met a huge bump crusted over with dried blood.

She touched it and moaned at the pain that ripped through her.

"Cairstine?" Greer asked. "You are alive? Cairstine, say something." He knelt next to her bed, his gaze searching hers, an unfamiliar expression on his face.

Greer appeared to be worried.

"What happened?" she whispered, afraid to speak too loudly because of the ache in her head.

"You fell against the wall and hit your head." He picked her up and set her on his lap, leaning back against the wall.

Bits and pieces came back to her. They'd been in the cellars, talking about Steenie and the crying she'd heard. He'd turned furious over her concern about the bairns, warning her never to speak of them again.

"You pushed me, Greer." She allowed her head to fall against his chest simply because pain shot down her neck when she tried to hold it upright. A moan ripped from her. "Where's Steenie? I want to see him. Please?"

"I'm sorry. Aye, I pushed you, but 'twas an accident. I thought you were as good as dead. Hilda said many die from blows to the head."

Was she mistaken or had she seen true concern on Greer's face? Was he capable of remorse? It didn't matter. She had to find out what had happened to her son. "Steenie? Where is he?"

Greer shouted, "Hilda? She needs you."

If he'd had any guilt or worry about her well-being, it quickly disappeared.

Hilda came inside, bustling over to the chest to mix a potion for her to drink. "This will make her feel better. Can you look at me, Cairstine?"

Cairstine lifted her gaze, as much as it pained her to move, up to Hilda's face.

"Good. She's looking at me straight on. 'Tis a good sign. If she can lift this potion to her lips on her own, I think she'll heal."

Hilda moved back to the chest to finish her concoction. "Here." She set the goblet in her hand. "Drink this. 'Twill make the throbbing ebb."

Greer grabbed it and lifted it to Cairstine's lips.

Hilda clucked her tongue. "See if she can do it, Greer. 'Tis how I'll know if she's better."

Cairstine did not care how it got to her lips, so she grabbed the goblet from him and swallowed it down, hoping it worked quickly. When she finished, she repeated herself, "Steenie, where is he?"

"We couldn't find him," Greer said, "but now that you're better, I'll go back out for him."

She lifted her gaze to Greer's again, wondering what had caused the change in his demeanor. If he were showing her some kindness, there had to be something in it for him. Did he actually feel guilty? Her head hurt too much to think on Greer and his motives. She needed to focus on Steenie. Where could he be? How could he have disappeared again so quickly?

"Nay…" she whispered, secretly praying her son had

escaped the Lamonts for good. She prayed Braden Grant
had come upon him and taken him home.

She closed her eyes and opened them again, surprised
to see Blair standing next to Greer. "Blair? Why are you
here?"

Distantly, she heard Greer say, "Blair's not here. Hilda,
what's wrong with her?"

"She's seeing double. 'Tis from the bump on her head
and the potion."

Only Hilda's words sounded even farther away, as if she
were deep in a long tunnel. She was quite sure she could
fall asleep and not be bothered by their conversation.

She sighed as the pain subsided enough for her to close
her eyes, and when she did, she wished she could sleep for
days.

———◆———

BRADEN, RODDY, AND LOKI JOINED the wee lads
in the hall. As the group settled at one of the trestle
tables with Steenie and Kenzie, Uncle Alex joined them.
He had heard about Loki's companion and had come
inside to chat with the boy.

Steenie had already polished off two meat pies and was
working on a pastry, licking the juice from his fingers.
"This is the best ever. May I have another, please? Mama
says if I say please, then I may have 'nother. Does that work
here, too?"

Uncle Alex sat in a chair and rested his feet on a nearby
bench. "Aye," he said. "Kenzie will find you another, but
first tell me about your keep. How many of you live there?"

Steenie set his pastry down and folded his hands on his
lap. "Who are you, my lord?"

Alex smirked as he answered the lad. "I'm Alexander
Grant. I used to be chieftain of the Grants, but now my
two eldest lads share the lairdship, though they're away at
the moment. That puts me back in charge."

Steenie's eyes widened. "You're the laird? My lord. My laird. What should I call you?"

"Call me Alex. 'Tis fine for now. Now about your castle…"

"I live with my mama and papa, and my uncle Blair. Blair is Papa's brother. The Lamont brothers, 'tis what the guards call them."

"And your mama?"

"She's called Cairstine, but she's locked up in the cellars. Will you get her out? I miss my mama. I'm probably not supposed to say that if I want to be a warrior. Papa says she coddles me."

Alex whispered, "Don't tell anyone, but I miss my mama every day. I wish she were still here to coddle me."

"You do?" The lad stared at Uncle Alex in disbelief, and Braden couldn't help but wonder if he was being honest. He guessed he was since he'd never known his uncle to tell anything but the truth.

"I do. And I miss my papa, too. He loved my mama verra much. He was verra kind to her."

Braden held his breath, knowing exactly what his uncle was doing, hoping to bait the lad into discussing his mother's treatment by his sire. His uncle never failed to impress him with his cleverness, but would Steenie be honest?

Steenie stared at his hands in his lap. "I miss my mama, but not Papa. He thrashes me all the time."

"Is your papa kind to your mama?"

Steenie's eyes teared up and he whispered, "Nay. He's always yelling at her. But he doesn't thrash her the way he does me. When he gets mad at her, he hits her in the face. He uses his fist with Mama. Sometimes he puts her in the cellars, like he did this time."

Then he surprised everyone by pointing to Braden. "He said men are not supposed to hit people smaller than them. Is that true, Alex?" He had the most serious expression Braden had ever seen on a child. He'd wondered what

Cairstine had been forced to deal with, but now he wondered about the lad, too. His life could not be easy.

"Aye, 'tis true. I never hit women or bairns. And you will not either, will you?"

His eyes widened and he shook his head furiously.

"Is your mama's name Cairstine Muir?"

He frowned and thought about the question for a few moments before he answered. "Nay, just Cairstine, but Mama tells me stories about the great Muirs. 'Tis the same? About their laird and mistress and the special holidays they celebrated. Do you mean those Muirs?"

"Aye, those Muirs. How old are you, Steenie?"

"Five winters," he replied, puffing his chest out a bit. "I'm old enough to help my mother now. Will you get her out of the cellars? Tell my da he cannot keep her there?"

"I will. I'll send some of our warriors out there to get her out of the cellars. Will that make you happy?"

"Aye," he said, bolting out of his seat. "Now? Can we go now?"

"Nay, we shall leave at dawn."

"But…but…"

"We'll get her freed, Steenie. I promise you."

Braden knew what was going through Steenie's mind, the same exact thing that was going through *his* mind.

He couldn't wait until dawn.

He was going after her tonight.

———◆———

CAIRSTINE WOKE UP, SURPRISED TO find herself back in the cellars. As soon as she sat up, she knew she hadn't dreamed the entire sequence because her head pounded furiously, just like before. Perhaps she'd only dreamed the bit about Greer expressing guilt over what he'd done. It had been the first time he'd shown remorse about anything.

Mayhap she'd been down here all along, not in her comfortable bed.

She'd never had a headache this bad before. Reaching her hand up to the side of her head, she moaned as soon as her fingers touched the large swelling, still crusted over with blood.

Steenie. Had they found Steenie yet?

She forced herself to stand, and while she was a wee bit wobbly, she managed to walk to the door in a straight line. Once there, she peeked through the window as best she could, searching for anyone.

"Hilda?"

As soon as the name left her mouth, her head throbbed again. "Ow."

"Lass, you're awake?" Hilda came rushing down the passageway from a distance away. "How do you feel?"

"My head is still causing me too much pain." She massaged her forehead to see if that would help, using the softest touch possible, but to no avail.

"I can give you more potion."

"Nay, nay. Not if it puts me to sleep again. Where's Steenie? Have they found him yet? Why am I back here? I thought Greer was being nice to me, though mayhap my head is addled."

"Nay, they have not found Steenie. Greer and Blair are both out looking for him. 'Tis why you're back down here. Greer was afraid you'd go out searching for the lad on your own if you were not contained, and 'twould not be safe for you. He thought it best to keep you locked up. He'll set you free when he returns."

"Why did he not leave me with you?" She placed her hand over her forehead, then leaned her hand against the bars in the small opening in the door, hoping to alleviate some of the stabbing pain in her head.

Hilda cupped her cheek through the window. "I'm sorry, but I have to leave. There is something I must do, and even though it bothers me something fierce, I have no choice in the matter." With that, she dropped her hand.

Cairstine recalled the crying bairns. True, Greer had told her never to mention it again, but Hilda would never betray her to him. "Hilda, I heard bairns crying down the hall before I was hurt. Who were they?"

Hilda jerked her gaze up to Cairstine, her surprise at the question quite obvious. Then she dropped her gaze again. "I cannot say, lass, and you do not want to know." Her eyes misted with tears and she whispered, "I wish I didn't. I must go."

With that, Hilda turned around and headed back down the passageway.

What could she be talking about?

Cairstine leaned her head against the wall but came up with no ideas. It just hurt too much to think. Footsteps echoed again in the passageway, and they grew louder. How she hoped this would be news about Steenie...

But alas, it was Corc who approached her. "I'm only here for a moment, lass, but I'm hoping to ease your mind. I never know when the Lamonts will return, so I have to make this visit short."

"Have they found him?"

"Nay, but I'm not worried."

"Why not? He's just a wee laddie. He doesn't know his way around out there." She closed her eyes, so afraid for her son.

"Lass, I'm telling you. Your son is stronger and braver than you think. He's mighty worried about you because he's seen evidence of Greer's temper. He told me he was going to go to the Grants someday, so he could ask them to come show his father how to be nice to you."

"He did?" How she adored her son. He had such a natural sweetness about him. How she prayed he'd never lose it. "Do you think 'tis where he went?"

"I do. I think he went to Grant land to get help for you. He doesn't like it when you're in the cellars. I know it's only been a couple of times, but it upsets him terribly." Corc chewed on a blade of straw stuck in the corner of his mouth.

"But what if he gets lost?" She rubbed her hands at the chill in the cellars, wishing she had another blanket. The one plaid wasn't quite warm enough for her.

The thought of Steenie out there alone made her ill, though she tried to think good thoughts. She said a quick prayer for the Lord to watch over her son. Many times, she thought her mother overheard her prayers. If she could, she and Cairstine's sire would watch over Steenie, too.

"Do you know how many patrols the Grants send out in a sennight? His men and his allies are all over Scotland. If not Alex Grant's men, it could be Loki Grant's warriors or Torrian Ramsay's, or the Drummonds or the Menzies. None of them would harm a child. They'll find him if he gets even close. Now, stop worrying your pretty head about him, and trust that the Lord will send the Grants out to find your son. *I* do."

"I think I recall the Grants visiting with Da. Would that have been Alex Grant?"

"Aye, the same. He used to bring his daughter and carry her on his shoulders. He had twin lads that were a wee bit wild."

"Do you know Braden Grant?"

"Nay, why do you ask?"

She stared at her hands for a moment, but since Greer was gone, there was no reason to worry. She trusted Corc completely. "I met him out the back when the Grants were here before. 'Tis why I'm down here. Greer thought we'd been speaking too close."

Corc stared off into space, scratching his head. "Alex's brothers are Brodie and Robbie. Mayhap Braden is a son to one of them. Any Grant would be a good man. Trust him."

"They won't hurt Steenie, will they?"

"Alex Grant is the biggest man I know, but he'd never hurt a bairn. I see you still have a bump on your head. Rest up, lass. The Grants are the strongest and most honorable clan in the Highlands. You can trust them. Now that I've checked on you, I must go back to the stables in case the brothers from hell return. Not to tempt fate, but 'tis finally time for things to change around here." He turned around and padded back down the passageway.

CHAPTER TWELVE

B RADEN DIDN'T TELL ANYONE THAT he planned to be gone long before morning. He would wait until dark and head over to Lamont land alone. He'd found his way to the back entrance before, so he'd do the same again. Though he was well aware that he could run into the Lamont brothers if they were out searching for Steenie, his will was unassailable.

He prepared himself for the journey in early evening. He'd already left one of the strongest horses in the stables outside the gates after he took him for a ride through the meadow and tied him up in the trees. His saddlebag was already filled with oatcakes, a spare plaid, and any other items he may need.

His sire caught up with him on one of his trips through the courtyard. "You look as though you're planning something, son."

Braden caught his sire's gaze, something different there than what he often saw—respect? Should he be honest with his sire?

His father said, "Never mind. I recall being young and foolish, just as you are. I was driven to save a beautiful lass from being tortured. Naught could have stopped me. Sound familiar?"

Braden nodded. "Aye, you saved Mama from a cruel Norseman."

"Aye. But I was lucky. With Nicol and Loki's help, I was able to save her." He paused for a moment, one eye closed, as he assessed Braden. Then he continued. "Learn from your sire and know that you cannot do it alone. Recognize when you must hold your tongue and your temper until you can get assistance. I couldn't have rescued your mama by myself."

Braden said, "I'll be traveling with Connor and Roddy on the morrow."

Brodie Grant chortled. "Will you, now? I know that look you have about you. I've seen it in the mirror before. Seen it on both of my brothers, and on my nephews. We Grants are impatient warriors. One more story for you, and I'll leave you to do what you must."

Braden took in his sire with a different look. Perhaps he had some wisdom of his own to impart. He'd always looked to Uncle Alex, but his sire had been through the Battle of Largs and survived, brought Loki home and adopted him. He owed him a bit more respect than he'd given him before. "I'm listening, Papa."

"The most foolish thing I did was after the Battle of Largs. I had a serious leg injury that needed tending by my sister, not some sad healer found in Ayr. Alex sent me home with Nicol and Uncle Logan. In fact, when Brenna saw it, she said if I'd been another day, she'd have had to cut my leg off above my knee."

Braden glanced down to his sire's legs. "But you got home in time. You still have it." Where was he going with this story? He didn't recall hearing this one before.

"Aye. I was out cold when I left Ayr, so I don't remember it, but I came to in the middle of the Highlands. I got up and promptly told Logan and Nicol I was going after Celestina, and they weren't going to stop me. I was in love with your mother and didn't wish to be without her.

"My determination took over and I stalked over to my horse and did my best to leave with the intent of going back for your mother, which would have taken at least another sennight."

"What stopped you?"

He smirked, dropping his head as the memories assailed him apparently. "For one thing, I couldn't mount the horse because my leg was in such bad shape, but that didn't stop me. I needed something a wee bit more forceful. Uncle Logan. I heard him say something about my sorry arse and then he punched me in the face, knocking me out. I never woke up until I was back at our keep. If not for those two, I'd only have one leg. So do your sire, your mother, and that young lady a favor and think before you let your stubbornness guide you. I wouldn't have been the same with only a stump for a leg. Who knows if your mama would even have had me then."

"She wouldn't have left you over losing your leg. Did you two not fall in love right away?"

His sire grinned. "Aye, I saw her on a balcony. I thought she was about to jump off. When I finally met her up close, I knew she was the one for me. 'Twas her scent and her eyes. I just couldn't forget either one. Uncle Alex said I hardly knew her, but I knew enough."

Braden had to admit he was stunned. "I never thought falling for someone happened that quickly."

"It does when 'tis right. 'Tis all I can tell you about it. You'll know. When you find yourself thinking of only one person and no one else and thoughts of having her in your arms overtake all other thoughts, 'tis time to admit that you've found the one. However, 'tis a dangerous situation to be in when you're headed into battle. Keep your head about you, lad. Do not allow that stubborn head of yours to get in the way."

"You think I have a temper and I'm stubborn, too?"

"Where do you think you get those qualities from?" His sire patted his shoulder and said, "Godspeed, wherever your journey takes you. Don't make me give your mother bad news." He walked away, a small smile still on his face.

With his sire's words fresh in his mind, he made his way out toward the gates, making sure to act normally and not draw any attention to himself. It would be dark in less than an hour, and he needed to be on his way by then. He did stop once to pause and glance back over his shoulder at his sire. If he really wanted to prevent Braden from leaving, he would have. Instead he was leaving the choice in his hands.

He ran into Steenie in the courtyard. The lad looked to have a similar intention as he had.

"Can we not leave now to free my mama?" The laddie looked up at him with such admiration and hope. How he wished to tell him that he planned to go after Cairstine himself and not wait until the morrow, but he couldn't.

"Trust the Grants to get your mama out. You'll want to be here to see the swarm of Highland warriors leaving for Lamont land. We'll have so many horses…"

"And swords." The boy yanked his own sword out and swung it around him a few times, not stopping until a voice called out to him.

"You need better training, Steenie," Kenzie said, his hands on his hips. "Come, I'll take you to our practice spot in the corner of the bailey. I'll show you how to fight like a Grant."

The two took off, Steenie's short legs going as fast as possible in his attempt to keep up with the older lad. It was nearly dark. Braden's patience was waning, so he decided to wait no longer. He walked straight across the courtyard and through the gates without being stopped. He was ready to leave.

He found his horse quietly munching on a rare group of thick grasses. He patted his flank just before he mounted. "We're off, my friend. You'll not fail me this night. We must save a lassie from a cruel overlord."

At one point on his journey, he was forced to hide in a copse of trees to elude several horses headed his way. He climbed a tree to get a better visual and was surprised to see both Lamont brothers traveling a distance away, headed in the opposite direction.

If he had to guess, he would say they were searching for a wee lad around five summers. He couldn't have planned it better. That would make it easy for him to enter the Muir Castle since there would be a reduced number of guards on duty. He doubted that was the only patrol out searching for Steenie.

Once the men were out of sight, he mounted and sent his horse into a gallop, heading straight for the back of the Lamont holding. That entrance was probably deserted, or so he hoped.

Sure enough, it was unguarded. Moving as quietly as possible, he slipped into the back entrance of the keep, made his way down the stairs, and began to search the cellars. He vowed not to stop until he found Cairstine.

Once he made it to the bottom of the stairs, he waited for his eyes to adjust to the darkness. There was only one torchlight in the passageway, so he headed in that direction, guessing it was near her cell.

He stopped outside the second door because he knew she was inside. He could sense her presence. There was something about the lass that would never leave him. Creeping over to the window in the door, he peeked inside and found her sitting on the pallet, her head in her hands. He located the key ring on the wall not far away and carefully removed the keys, not wanting the sharp jingling of metal to alert anyone to what he was doing. All was quiet in the hall above, so he guessed the remaining guards were either imbibing or patrolling the curtain wall and protecting the gates.

———◆———

CAIRSTINE JUMPED OFF THE BED as soon as she heard the key in the lock, wondering who she would see on the other side. Greer had said he was off to search for Steenie, and he hadn't been gone long.

Or at least she didn't think so.

Instead, Braden Grant stood in front of her just inside the doorway. She couldn't have been more shocked to see him.

"My lady." He nodded to her but otherwise stayed put.

She had no idea what to say to him. "I'm no lady," was the only thing that popped into her mind.

"You are the daughter of the Muir. Thus, you are a lady, whether you wish to deny it or not."

"I don't deny he was my sire," she managed to get out before the tears flooded her cheeks. "But I'm no longer a lady. I am an unmarried woman with a child. A wench."

Braden took two slow steps toward her until he stood an arm's length away. "Nay. Wench is not the word for you at all. Victim or captive comes to mind. Did you request to stay with the Lamonts after they massacred your family?"

"How could you even suggest such a thing?" she whispered. She'd tried so hard to block out memories of that night, but it always returned.

"Your sire was the laird of the Muirs, your mother lived in this keep along with you and your brother. The Lamonts came along and took your sire by surprise, murdering all but you because one of them, I'm guessing Greer, wished to use you for his own pleasures. Am I correct?"

She turned her head away as the tears came out in a torrent. Unable to speak, all she could do was nod, acknowledging that he'd added up the pieces correctly. She hung her head in shame.

He took two steps closer and placed his finger under her chin, lifting her gaze to meet his, even as sobs wracked her body. "You are a lady, Cairstine Muir. You have survived rape, brutal torture, and you've kept your son alive. To me, that speaks of a verra strong woman, not a wench."

"What do you want? You know I cannot go with you.

My son will be brought back here. At least I hope so." She wrapped her arms around her waist, as though hugging herself would make the pain go away.

"Nay, he won't. He's safely on Grant land. He found his way out of here on his own, and my brother Loki brought him to Grant Castle. Greer and Blair are out searching for him, so there could be no better time for you to leave."

"He's free? Truly free? He's with the Grants and you'll protect him from Greer Lamont?" She could hardly grasp the reality of what he was saying. Could the two of them get away and live a normal life together—away from the Lamonts?

"Aye, we will."

"But Greer is his sire. Does that not carry rights to all? Can he not go claim Steenie?"

"Trust me, my brother Loki will not return him after all your son told us. Loki is the protector of all bairns in the Highlands. He'll protect Steenie with his life."

Hope sparked in her heart, golden and precious and new, but hope was a dangerous thing. What if he was toying with her? Could she believe him? What if he was lying about Steenie?

She shook her head and took a step back, though the tears fell unencumbered down her cheeks and onto her gown.

"You call me a lady. Do ladies wear gowns like this?" she asked, holding the coarse wool out for him to see. "Do ladies sleep in chambers such as this one? Are ladies kept away from their sons? Are they kept hidden so they have no idea where their lads are?"

How could she possibly trust this man?

Because he held you once and never hurt you. Because he's come for you again. For some reason the thought popped into her mind in the voice of her mother.

How she wished her mother could truly send her advice. *I don't know what to do, Mama. I miss you so much.*

"May I beg you to trust me for one minute?" he asked without moving any closer.

"Nay." She shook her head vehemently and swiped at the tears still drenching her cheeks. "You'll want to rut on me just like the bastards who killed my clan. No more. And how can I trust what you say about Steenie?"

Nay, he'll not, child. Trust him. Her mother's voice called to her again, the sweetness of the timbre causing an ache in her heart, yet she begged to hear it again. A lump formed in her throat that she couldn't clear.

We chose him for you, Cairie.

She sobbed and gasped at the memory of her mother's favorite name for her when she was just a wee lass. No one else ever called her that. Was it possible that her mother could be speaking to her now?

He took a step toward her. "I'm sorry for all the troubles fate has dealt you. If I have my way, Greer Lamont will pay for what he did to you and your clan. Can you please trust me for just one minute? I know what I'm asking of you."

She thought of her mother's words and nodded. How she wanted to be able to trust this man, to believe that he would take her away and bring her to her dear son. No matter how she tried, she couldn't stop the tears. What could he possibly do in one minute? "Go ahead," she hitched. "One minute." She stiffened in fear but vowed to give him a chance.

His hand reached out and his thumb swiped a tear away with the softest touch she'd ever felt.

His dark gaze locked on hers, those soulful eyes that called to her. "The problem is you were taken captive at such a young age that you've not been around many good men. I'm not about hurting women. My sire raised me to respect women—in fact, 'tis important to all the Grants." The back of his fingers brushed against her cheek, then down her neck and arm until he reached her hand. His hand wrapped around hers and he cocooned his hands around hers, lifting her fingers to his lips before he proceeded to kiss each finger. Gently releasing her hand, he cradled her cheek with his palm. He caught one of her tears and brought it to his own lips, tasting the drop of liquid with his tongue.

Her hand trembled, as if one part of her wished to reach for him and the other wished to run away. She allowed herself the small pleasure of enjoying the warmth of his touch. What was it about Braden Grant that was different?

"I'd not have you crying if you were mine. I know how to treat a woman kindly. My mother was abused by a cruel man. I would never touch a woman in anger."

Then he did the oddest thing. He cupped her cheek with one hand and asked her a question. "May I kiss you?"

She nodded, wanting the words that had echoed in her mind to be true, that those words would have come from her beloved mother and father. How she wished they had chosen this man to save her. She knew her mind could be playing trickery with her, but she wanted Braden Grant to save her, to help her and Steenie. He was honorable and trustworthy. She knew it in her heart. This was the third time she'd seen him, and he'd never forced anything on her.

He settled his lips on hers in a gentle way totally foreign to her. Whereas Greer's attentions were always rough and punishing, his teeth knocking into hers in his violence, Braden's lips were soft and warm. He angled his mouth over hers and touched his tongue to the seam of her lips, encouraging her to part them, and she gave in, some strange force within her wishing to see how different things could be, how a relationship was supposed to be.

His tongue tasted her in a way that made her want more, so much so that she touched the tip of her tongue to his. He teased her tongue until they dueled a bit and he groaned, tugging her closer, wrapping his arms around her in a way that made her feel protected, desired, and special.

He ended the kiss and she stared up at him in awe.

There was nothing brutal about this man. Instead she saw an honest, honorable man. Could she be wrong?

How she wished to believe in him. She'd never been touched the way he touched her, as though she were the most precious person in all of Scotland. His eyes were truthful, soulful, and so incredibly warm. She stepped back from him, wishing to regain some clarity of thought. "Steenie? How do I know you're being truthful?"

"One of the things he loves the most is when you tell him about the special Muir holidays of your childhood. 'Tis something he shared with me."

Only Steenie would know that truth. She'd told him stories when she knew no one else could overhear them. Refusing to forget her parents and her heritage, she'd done her best to instill some of it in her son without telling him about their death.

This had come from her son. He was with the Grants. Her inner will crumbled.

She leaned toward him and he opened his arms for her, gathering her close as she fell against him, tucking her head under his chin. Steenie, Hilda, and Corc were the only ones she could talk to about her family, so she knew he told the truth. Her son was safely away from Greer Lamont. A torrent of sobs gushed out of her, and she clung to him as if she never wanted to let him go.

He held her until she had no sobs left inside her, rocking her just a bit. A few moments later, he kissed her forehead and said, "We need to go. I know not when the Lamonts will return. I'd like to get you away from here now. Trust me? Please?"

How could she not? He was the one man who could take her to her son.

"I trust you."

He led her out of the chamber and down the passageway, but life had a way of keeping her from any happiness. As soon as they opened the back door in the curtain wall and stepped into the land behind the keep, a voice called out to them.

Greer bellowed, "Cairstine. Where are you? I'll find you, you filthy wench!"

CHAPTER THIRTEEN

———————

STEENIE AND KENZIE PRACTICED WITH their swords until it was too dark to see anymore.

"Kenzie, you are the best swordsman of all," Steenie declared. "Now I am a warrior just like you. And I'm ready to save my mama!"

He sheathed his sword and ran toward the gates.

Kenzie shouted after him as he chased across the bailey. "Where are you going?"

"I must find my pony, Paddy."

The wee lad's legs churned faster than should have been possible as he found his pony outside the stables. Several guards had just come in from patrol and they were mumbling about something and hurrying up to the hall, so the stable lads were busy taking care of their horses. They paid him no mind. He stood on a block and saddled his pet, then mounted just before Kenzie came around the corner. When he came charging out of the stables, there was no one there to stop him.

"Where are you going, Steenie?" Kenzie yelled again.

"To save my mama," he replied. He held his sword in the air, nearly fell off Paddy, then sheathed it and spurred his pony onward.

"You cannot go alone," Kenzie shouted.

Steenie glanced over his shoulder as he rode through the gates. He heard Kenzie shouting to his sire, "Papa, Steenie is trying to go after his mama. We must go with him."

That was the last thing he heard. He was outside the Grant keep, urging Paddy into a nice gallop. After a short time, he heard horses following him, so he found a hiding spot where no one would find him. Several patrols raced by him, but then he snuck out again with a giggle. He wouldn't allow anyone to stop him, not even the mighty Grants.

"Come, Paddy. We'll rescue Mama," he whispered as he patted his dear friend.

He hadn't gone far when a horse pulled out in front of him, catching him off guard. The lad on the horse said, "Where do you think you're going?"

He breathed a sigh of relief when he saw it was only Kenzie. "Come with me. We have to help her now. We can't wait."

Paddy tossed his head back with a whinny as if he was upset to be slowed on their journey. Steenie leaned over him to give him a hug. "Paddy is my new friend and he's going to help me, even if you'll not, Kenzie."

Kenzie sighed and said, "I couldn't find my sire. We really should wait for my papa to come along and help us."

"I cannot wait for him. My mama needs me now. I know it." He held his sword up again for emphasis. He liked handling it like the Grant guards did. Papa would be impressed, and surely he would be persuaded to listen.

Kenzie glanced over his shoulder. "All right. I'll go with you."

"Don't come if you're scared. I'm not going back without Mama," Steenie said, pointing his sword at Kenzie. "Mayhap you need to stay behind." He lifted his chin to let Kenzie know he was serious before he resheathed his weapon and tugged on Paddy's reins. "Come, Paddy. Lead the way to my mama."

Kenzie let out a huge sigh and pouted. "Go ahead. I'll not stop you, but I will follow close behind. Just be careful.

I don't want a thrashing either."

"Does your papa thrash you, too?"

Kenzie snorted. "Nay, but he threatens often. And this is definitely a thrash-worthy offense."

———◆———

BRADEN AND CAIRSTINE DIDN'T GET far before they were dragged back into the great hall by a dozen Lamont men.

Greer grabbed Cairstine while Blair and two others held on to Braden.

"You were going to leave me, weren't you? Even though I feed you, clothe you, keep a roof over your head, gave you a son, you would take off with another man, you slut. I'll teach you who owns you." His hand swung out and caught her across the face. "You're staying with me, but you'll no longer have the luxurious treatment you're used to. Nay, this time you'll get what you deserved all along."

He slapped her again. Hard.

So hard that he had to catch her to keep her from falling, her hands going up to protect her head.

Braden noticed the swelling through her hair that he hadn't seen before. "She has a head injury and you hit her again, you piece of shite?" Braden thought his own head would explode. "I'll kill you with my bare hands when I'm free, Lamont."

Greer chuckled. "I doubt you'll ever be free to carry out your promise, Grant. What interest have you with my woman?"

Braden spat on the floor. "Your woman? You care for her so much that you never married her? Raped her and got her with child? Did you give her to your brother, too, arsehole?"

Greer glanced at Blair. "He's funny, is he not? Blair, do me a favor and find the lad. Send him along with the others going on the journey."

Blair nodded but said nothing, glancing at Cairstine before he left.

Greer put his hand around Cairstine's waist and tugged her to him so her back was against his chest. He moved in close so his lips were next to her ear, "You will regret whoring for another man. Am I not good enough for you?"

He grabbed her hair and yanked. "Answer me! Why were you trying to leave me? Am I not good enough to lie between your legs, wench?"

Braden could see Cairstine grit her teeth as the man tugged harder on her hair. How the hell had she survived six years with this scum? "Stay strong, Cairstine. I'll get you away from him."

"Answer me," he ground out. "Or I'll take you right here in front of your new friend."

"Greer, you put me back in the cellars and locked the door," she shouted as he yanked on her hair again. "You're always holding me back, just like you are now."

He gave her a push over toward Braden, but she didn't move. "You want the man with the red plaid? You can go with him. I'll let the two of you leave." He began to pace, something that pleased Braden. He'd unsettled the bastard.

The man surely didn't intend to allow them to leave. He was playing mind games with Cairstine. Braden knew better than to believe him, but did she?

One of the guards dropped his hands from Braden's arm and nodded to the other one restraining him. Both of them let him go. He shook his arms because the little movement kept him from swinging at all the daft fools the way he wished to do. Roddy's warnings stayed in his mind. His temper flared, and all he wished to do was beat that bastard to a pulp, but he took two deep breaths to rein it in. It was one man against at least a dozen. He needed to be calm and collected for Cairstine in order to get them out of the castle safely. He needed to be more like his uncle.

Restraint nearly killed him, but he thought of his sire's words and held his tongue and his fists.

Cairstine stood between the two men, clearly torn. Aye, she knew better than to trust Greer at his word.

Greer crossed his arms in front. "Go ahead. Leave with him. I'll let you go. I've had enough of your whining. I'll find another pair of thighs to sink into, and it won't take me long."

"Where's Steenie?" she suddenly asked, keeping her gaze on Braden rather than Greer. Mayhap she was wondering if he'd lied…or she might simply know Greer enough to guess what he was about.

"*My* son? If you walk away, you'll not see him again, I can promise you that. I'll be certain to tell Steenie that you have no interest in him at all. That you left him willingly."

Braden held his hand out to Cairstine, then walked over to her when she didn't respond. "Believe me, Cairstine. He's safe at Grant Castle. Do not listen to him. He's taunting you with words. Come with me and I'll take you to the lad."

She gazed up at him with such hope in her eyes, his knees nearly buckled. How he wished he could make this woman's life better, that he would be given the chance to love her and show her how a woman should be treated. But she had to trust him first, and he knew trust could be a difficult thing to earn from an abused woman.

"Steenie's at Grant Castle?" Greer asked, cocking his head. "Why, that's odd. We found him out and about with another lad. Isn't that right?" He turned to one of his guards who nodded in agreement. "What was the name of the lad who was kindly escorting him home? 'Twas a new friend," he said. "Do you recall?"

Braden's heart began to race in fear. Who the hell had he grabbed?

Nay, he had to be bluffing. He had no name. He kept his gaze locked on Cairstine's, hoping to convey the message that he would help her find Steenie even if the lad wasn't at Grant Castle. If one of their own was missing, Clan Grant warriors would search the entire Highlands for him. But she wouldn't know that. He saw the tears misting her eyes, knew that she was about to cave in to this fool's theatrics.

The guard replied, "I think it was Kendell, Kenneth? Something like that. Or maybe Kennie?"

Shite. He tried not to let his worry show, but he failed because he saw his fear reflected in her eyes. The bastard had something he was planning, but he had to focus on getting her away from here. Steenie was not here, so she needed to go with Braden. He'd worry about Lamont's intentions later. *Don't give in to him.*

Greer clapped his hands. "Och, you're right. His name was Kenzie. Nice lad around ten summers, I'd guess. But as I said. Steenie is clearly none of your concern any longer. You're free to carry on as you wish at Grant Castle."

He could see the fine tremors in her hands. Lamont was going to force her to make a choice. How he prayed she'd make the right one, but he would understand if she couldn't. If the Lamonts had done anything with Kenzie and Steenie, the Grants were probably coming for them already, but she wouldn't understand that. The only thoughts in her mind at present were about keeping her son safe. He couldn't fight that.

Cruelty was all she'd known for the past six years.

"Go with him, Cairstine. Go with him and give up your son. I'll take good care of him. I already have. I just sent him on a little journey with Blair, as a matter of fact."

Cairstine asked, "Where is he, Greer? If he were here, I would know it."

"He's hidden, well hidden. And he'll soon be far away from here."

Her hands shook, but she reached for Braden's hand. Relief showered over him as he wrapped his arm around her waist and led her over to the door. "We'll find him," he whispered, speaking low enough so she was the only one to hear him.

"Oh, Cairstine? I forgot to tell you. Do you remember the question you asked me when you were in the cellar? The noises you heard? They've all gone now, and they're headed far away from here. No need to worry about the bairns anymore."

She froze and pulled her hand out of Braden's, turning her head toward the areshole with wide eyes. "What did you do, Greer?"

"What is it?" Braden asked.

"They're no longer your concern," Greer added. Just know that I added two more to travel with them. Steenie and his new friend, Kenzie, isn't that right, Grant? It's just a pity you won't be able to say goodbye, but I'm sure he'll grow into a fine man in time; that is, after he forgets his years of servitude, if he makes it past them."

She pivoted, a slow turn, horror written on her face. Braden had no idea what the man was talking about, though if he had to guess, it sounded much like the Channel of Dubh. Anything that concerned innocent bairns or servitude brought to mind the secret network that Maggie and Will were trying to pinpoint and shut down.

Braden said, "Sounds as if you're involved in something that you may regret. Where are the bairns headed?"

Lamont ignored him.

"What did you do, Greer?"

"It's not what I did do, but what I will do. You're more interested in spreading your legs than raising the lad, and I'll not raise him myself, so I have no other choice. But by all means, go with your new man and forget about Steenie. He knows you've deserted him. Poor lad cried something awful when I told him you'd left without him. But if you wish to see him, I *could* take you there. Mayhap I'd even change my mind."

"Take me to Steenie." Cairstine insisted at once.

"Cairstine, nay. I know of what he speaks, and I'll help you find him." Braden clenched his fists, doing his best to hold his temper and not start swinging. He was outnumbered, and besides, he wouldn't risk Cairstine getting hurt in a scuffle.

"Take me to Steenie." Her voice was strong, and he was proud of her. She loved her son. He'd never fault her for her undying devotion to her bairn.

Braden had to keep her focused. Didn't she understand the strength of Clan Grant? "Don't believe him, Cairstine. He wouldn't do that to his own son."

"Wouldn't I? She watched me plunge my dagger straight into her mother's heart. She knows I have no conscience. Do you know what else she saw, Grant? Something verra few people get to see." His eyes lit up with sick glee over whatever he was about to reveal. The man was a twisted bastard.

Braden glanced at Cairstine and reached for her hand, but she tugged away from him, tears now flowing freely down her cheeks. The door opened and Blair strode back in, alone.

"Her brother came straight at me after we'd killed her father. The big lout thought he'd kill me, but he was wrong, wasn't he, Blair?"

Blair laughed but said nothing.

Braden did his best to distract Greer. "Where did you send the bairns, Lamont? Do you have any idea what you're involved with?"

Blair jerked his head around to his brother. "What the hell did you tell him, Greer?"

Greer rolled his eyes at his brother. "Naught that matters. He has no idea what we're about. He's guessing, doing his best to persuade Cairstine to leave me." He turned his back to his brother to return to Cairstine. "You recall how your brother died, aye? You saw me kill two of your family and it didn't bother me. Do you think I'll be bothered by killing you, or Grant? Or Steenie? He's just another mouth to feed." He waved his hand toward Braden. "Go ahead. Go with him. Make your choice."

She stared at Braden, now sobbing, "My brother loved our papa that much. Said he'd get revenge for their deaths." Her breath hitched, and the last words came out in a wail. "You know how I hate you, Greer. I only stay for one reason. For Steenie. I cannot leave him. He's all I have."

Braden had no words. What could he say to someone who'd watched her parents and brother murdered? She had to fear for her life every day.

"Take me to Steenie, Greer." She turned around and walked over to him. "I'm sorry. I've changed my mind. I'll stay."

Greer glared at her, his arms still crossed. "Convince me."

Braden had walked over to the door, ready to leave and summon all the force of the Grants, when Greer called out to him. "Hold, Grant."

Braden turned around and waited. He was so pissed at the power the arsehole had over Cairstine that he just wanted to do something about it, but he understood. He wished she could trust him, but they barely knew each other. How he wanted to walk away, but his training as a Grant warrior forced him to lift his chin with pride. There was still a slim possibility she could change her mind, and he refused to give up on her. How he admired her with all she'd dealt with. A lesser woman would have crumpled to the ground in defeat long ago.

Greer said, "Convince me, Cairstine. Spit on him."

"Nay, Greer," Cairstine said. "I'll not do it."

"Do it. Spit on him or I'll have him killed."

"*Bastart*," she cried out.

Greer grinned.

She strode over to stand in front of Braden and mouthed two words out of Greer's view. "I'm sorry."

Then she spat on him.

Greer nodded to his men. "Take him outside and rough him up. Then give him his sword and drop him in the middle of the forest without his horse. Send the Grants a message that the Lamonts will not be easily toyed with."

Braden fought with every bit of strength he possessed, and though he took fist after fist in the courtyard, he gave back as many hits as were landed on his flesh.

He never felt a single blow. The pain of knowing Cairstine was still in that man's custody hurt more than any fist ever could.

CHAPTER FOURTEEN

———◆———

STEENIE STARED IN SHOCK AT all the lassies. Many were about his age. An old woman was busy preparing food for them in another chamber. He'd only seen her from behind because he couldn't take his gaze off the mean men in charge, but they'd just left in a hurry, telling the woman they'd be moving again by nightfall.

He leaned over to whisper to Kenzie. "Who are all these bairns? Where are they taking us?" He heard one of the lassies cry for her mother.

He was about ready to cry with her. He wanted his mama, too.

Kenzie said, "I think we're in the channel my papa told me about. His cousins know all about it."

"A channel to where?"

Kenzie sighed and locked gazes on him, holding his finger to his lips to urge him to keep quiet. "The river."

Steenie almost yelled, but Kenzie grabbed his shoulders. Steenie asked, "They're going to throw us in the firth?"

"Nay, they'll put us on a boat. We have to find a way out of this. All the Grant warriors will be searching for us, but we're hidden. There are no windows. 'Tis so dark I don't know what time of day 'tis."

Steenie said, "We're the warriors here. We must do something. We must hurt the mean one who's keeping us here."

Kenzie frowned at him. "We cannot hit her. She's a

woman. Grants do not hit women," Kenzie said. "Even bad ones."

One of the men walked inside and spoke to her.

"But we could hit him. Then she'd be scared of us," Steenie whispered. "Besides, we have to save all those lassies over there."

Kenzie said, "Mayhap we can try. I'll distract her when she comes back in, and you can hit him in the head."

"I'm not big enough." He swung his arm in imitation of what Kenzie needed to do. "You're bigger than me. You must be the one to strike him. And do it hard." He nodded for emphasis.

"Not a bad idea. You distract her and I'll take care of him." Kenzie glanced around the chamber. "I don't see anything I can use."

"I'll look."

Steenie moved around the small chamber. The four lassies around his age sat on a pallet on the floor, and they all looked as though they had been crying. One had just stopped as he approached them. Another had her thumb in her mouth. An older lassie sat on either side of the young ones, as if they'd decided to protect them.

"Who are you?" the one on the left asked.

"Steenie. We're going to save everyone. We need to find something to hit someone on the head with. Have you seen anything?"

"Here." After glancing about to ensure they weren't being watched, she moved over to a nearby stool and pulled one leg off. "This one was loose. Will it work?"

He nodded, grabbed it, and said, "Aye." He raced back over to Kenzie and said, "Here. When you hear her coming, hit him over the head with this."

Kenzie took the wooden leg and turned it over in his hand. "This could work."

"Here they come!" Steenie crept over to the doorway, pointing to the other side of the door where Kenzie could hide.

He was so nervous he thought his eyes would pop out of his head and roll onto the floor. He started to giggle at the idea of seeing such a thing when Kenzie said, "Pay attention, Steenie. You're supposed to distract the woman."

She was almost to the door so he stood up straight. He planned to fall down to draw her attention, and if that didn't work, he'd simply scream. He almost laughed at that, but then the door opened.

He took one look and said to Kenzie, "Nay! I know her and the bad man went back out."

Kenzie gave him a strange look, but he dropped the piece of wood as Steenie rushed forward and hugged the woman carrying a loaf of bread.

"Hilda. 'Tis you." He turned to Kenzie with a smile of relief on his face and said, "Don't worry. We're safe now.

———————

WHEN BRADEN OPENED HIS EYES, he had no idea where he was or what had happened. The sun was nearly up, so he knew a few hours had passed. He'd just pushed his hand against the cold ground when a boot nudged his shoulder.

"Got your arse kicked, brother?"

It had to be Loki. He groaned as he sat up, feeling as though he'd been tossed over a cliff and then dragged back up again. "What the hell?" Three sets of boots met his gaze, and he looked up just as Maggie Ramsay knelt down in front of him.

"What happened? The Lamonts?" She held out a skin for a drink.

"How'd you two get here so quickly? Uncle Alex just sent a missive to your sire."

Maggie said, "We met up with him. We were on our way because of ramblings we heard in Edinburgh about part of the Channel of Dubh that had been operating in the Highlands. We wanted to talk to your sire and uncles about deserted land. See if we could uncover anything, but it seems you've done much of our work for us, nay?"

Braden rubbed the blood crusted in his eyebrow, hoping the movement would brush the remaining cobwebs out of his brain. Cairstine. And Greer Lamont.

"Aye, you could say that." He took a swig, coughed a bit, then took another before he handed it back to her. Loki grabbed one of his arms and nodded to the pair of boots on Maggie's other side. *Will.* The two of them hoisted Braden to his feet.

"My thanks," Braden said. Glancing around the area and rubbing his head, he tried to place himself but finally decided it wasn't worth it. It was just too painful.

"They have Kenzie and Steenie. Where did they go?" Loki asked. "We have to find them fast."

"And Cairstine. That brute threatened her. Said he sold Kenzie and Steenie and other bairns. Somewhere they'd never find them. Tell me again what you heard in Edinburgh?" He glanced from Maggie to Will.

"We found out the Channel of Dubh operates a route running from this area to the Firth of Clyde. Seems to me these Lamonts must have gotten wrapped up in it," Will said. "We've heard they have no way of making income, so that would explain how they've been surviving all this time, and it doesn't seem they have any morals to speak of."

Braden said, "Aye, the same thought occurred to me, and after what I just heard, there's no doubt they are involved. Greer said he was sending the bairns away, along with Kenzie, that they'd never be seen again, but I think there's more to it. He said something to Cairstine about bairns crying in the cellars when she was locked up." He pulled all the twigs out of his hair that he could find. "He must have been holding them for some reason. What else but the Channel?"

Loki said, "If they know something, then we have to go

after them first. Since you were inside, any suggestions for how we should go in?"

"Where are the fifty warriors my sire promised? And Connor and Roddy?"

"Their group is coming behind us. I couldn't wait with Kenzie missing," Loki said. "I ran into these two and decided to bring them along."

Braden found a log to sit on before he continued. "I think we need to split up. I'll take a few back to the Lamonts with me, and the rest can look for the bairns. Where are Keith and Moray? They didn't come along?"

"Nay, said they'd prefer to stay back."

Braden closed his eyes. He'd have to worry about that situation later. He opened them and said, "If you wish to wait for the warriors, you may, but I'm not wasting any time. We need Cairstine's help. We need to stop Greer from doing away with the lads."

"If he sold them into the Channel of Dubh, then there may not be a way to find them," Maggie said. "Greer must be bluffing. Did he need to lie in order to convince Cairstine to stay?"

Braden nodded, working his shoulder because of a blow he took there. He needed to be in top form, and though he wasn't at present, he wouldn't let it stop him.

Loki whispered, "You going to be hale enough to go with us? Mayhap you should head back to Grant land and leave the rest to us."

"Hellfire, nay!" he glared at his brother, who grinned.

"Still works, doesn't it? Is that what got you beat up?"

Maggie asked, "What are you talking about?"

"Braden has a wee temper…"

"And I controlled it quite well, or I would be worse off and some of the Lamont guards would be dead. I controlled myself, but 'twas the hardest thing I've ever done," he barked at his brother.

"Can you *keep* that temper under control for the rest of

the journey?" Will asked.

"I'll be fine," he said with a sigh. "I have enough of a headache to keep me from yelling. But I can't do this alone so I'm asking for a few to go along with me to the Lamonts."

Maggie added, "We'll go with you. Loki, why don't you wait for the rest of the guards, then take your men and head straight for the waterways to the west. We'll join you when we're done."

The sound of horse hooves greeted them. They unsheathed their weapons to ready themselves for the newcomers, but the bird whistle in the early morning air quickly informed them it was Gavin and Gregor.

To their surprise, Connor and Roddy rode directly behind them with about forty more Grant guards, but the man in the middle of the group wore an unfamiliar plaid.

Loki tipped his head toward the gray-haired man on the horse. "Name? Never seen you before."

"You'll be pleased," Connor said with a grin. "Someone from inside the Lamonts."

Braden moved closer. "Why would we trust you?" He spat out a stream of spit and blood. "The Lamonts are no friend of the Grants or any clan in the Highlands."

"Nay, but I'm not a Lamont. My name's Corc from Clan Muir. I stayed on after the Lamonts slayed the Muirs. I was the stablemaster. Still am. But I saw them send the lads away. They'd always threatened to hurt Cairstine if I ever left, but the Lamonts have gone daft." He pointed to Braden. "After I saw what they did to you and saw them escort the lads from the keep, I decided to head to the Grants and hope you could find the bairns and get to Cairstine before they hurt her."

Braden couldn't believe their good fortune. This was another witness to the Lamonts' evil deeds.

"Don't know why the Lamonts spared me, but I stayed for Cairstine. Her sire would have wanted me to keep an eye on her. I couldn't do much to help her, but I've done aught I could. I cannot stand by any longer. I'm here to tell you I know where they took the bairns."

All faces turned toward him. Maggie asked, "Why would we trust you?"

"I promised Cairstine I'd keep an eye on Steenie. When they went out searching for the lad, I volunteered to help, and they allowed it. They sold the two lads to a small group who are taking a bunch of lassies to a boat in a loch in the west. That boat will bring them to the firth to put them on a larger boat headed across the waters. Steenie and another lad were added late, brought along on horseback."

"You can lead us there? Loki asked. "You're sure of the directions?"

"Aye. I paid close attention and tracked the path most of the way. A word of warning. We cannot wait long. If we miss the holding spot, we'll have to head west to the loch."

"How many men?"

"I saw four plus a woman to care for them. But she's been with the Lamonts for years and has a soft spot for the lad. She'll help the bairns if she can."

Braden asked, "Corc, you are willing to tell our king you witnessed both the Lamont brothers kill the Muirs?"

"Aye, I'll be glad to repeat all that I've witnessed."

"Tell us aught you can about where they left them," Maggie said. "You can lead Loki's group, and we'll follow. But Loki? I would head straight for the loch. Don't bother to stop at the holding spot. They will have been moved by now and they usually transport the bairns in slow carts. You'll be able to catch them."

Will said, "Terrific. We'll take the Band of Cousins with us to the castle. We'll finish here as quickly as we can and meet you at the loch."

"I'll give you two dozen guards if you want them," Loki said.

Maggie shook her head. "You may need them. I know

not how many they may have at the loading dock. There could be others escorting bairns there."

"We have nearly fifty with all of us," Loki said. "I'm sending two dozen guards to join you whether you want them or not. Order them to search the periphery, catch those who'll run before they fight, whatever, but I'm sending them. I'll not be able to leave if I know that your numbers are less than ten against Lamonts' fifty plus." He moved away to speak to his men, giving directions.

The two groups separated, but before their group rode off toward the castle, Maggie gave orders to the extra guards then pulled the rest of them together. "The situation, Braden. Fill everyone in."

"Greer and Blair Lamont slaughtered the Muirs six years ago," Braden said. "Kept the daughter, Cairstine, captive, and you can imagine how her life has been. They have possibly fifty to sixty guards. I want Greer."

Will said, "He's all yours. Is he the one who claims he knew how the channel operated?"

"Aye, but I think he's likely bluffing."

Will gave instructions. "We're going in through the front. No sense in trying to hide. Maggie has the others to take out anyone who gets past us. Direct is best because time is of the essence if we're to find the lads before the crossing. I don't think the Lamonts will have any information as I'd guess they've sent them to the loading station a while ago. But there could be other bairns here besides the two lads. We don't know anything for sure. Even they could possibly still be here."

Connor said, "Will, I might add that my sire wanted us on patrol, not a full-scale attack unless we knew that the Lamonts killed the Muirs or that they were holding bairns hostage. Do we all agree this mission has met both those criteria? Are we sure the king will see it that way?"

Will said, "Aye, without a doubt. Corc said he would speak as a witness, and he and Braden both spoke about the Channel. If the Lamonts are still here, once we find out what we can, a full-scale attack is warranted to end this blight on the Highlands."

Maggie nodded emphatically.

Braden said, "Rather than a direct attack, I have a better idea. Why not allow me to approach the gates alone? They all know me there, and I think I can lure Greer and Blair to come out and greet me. They won't perceive me as a threat. Especially in the sorry state they put me in. This way the two of them will be easily accessible and I can get the answers to our questions before we encounter the other guards. The rest of our men can hold back out of sight until the battle starts and the rest of Lamont's men come out of the gates. If I can go ahead of you, I may be able to determine exactly where Cairstine is, also. I'd like to get her to safety before the fighting begins in earnest."

Will rubbed his chin for a moment, considering his suggestion.

Maggie turned to him and said, "We can send Gavin and Gregor in ahead of Braden to position themselves. I'll go with them. That'll be three archers who can assist Braden if anything goes awry."

"Agreed. The full-scale attack ensues after we've drawn the Lamonts out?"

Maggie nodded. "Aye. Allow Braden to question them first, he can take on Greer if he wishes, then we can follow. Let's move."

Braden waited until she left before he moved into the bushes to take a pish.

Roddy teased him, "That's what you've been concentrating so hard on all this time?"

Braden came back with a smirk on his face. "Nay, but if I don't keep myself busy, I'll have a hard time holding back before battle."

He glanced up at the trees overhead. "And I have a strange feeling we won't be stopping once the Lamonts step outside their gates. You can be sure that I won't stop until Cairstine is safe."

CHAPTER FIFTEEN

———◆———

CAIRSTINE HAD BEGGED GREER NOT to kill Braden, but he'd only laughed, forcing her to watch, screaming and crying, as the men beat him until he was unconscious. The only bit of compassion they'd exercised was to leave him breathing.

She wondered if he would live. Greer had admitted the only reason he hadn't ordered his men to kill Braden was because he wanted him to remember it was Greer Lamont who'd humbled him. He wanted all the Grants to know what he was capable of doing to them.

She'd asked to be taken to Steenie, but Greer must have lied to her, because he'd given her no indication that he knew where her son was being held. Clearly, she had chosen the wrong man to trust. Time and experience should have taught her better, but she was blinded by the desperation to be reunited with her sweet boy.

When Greer had left the great hall to scavenge in the kitchens, she'd overheard Blair make a comment to him. "I can't believe you'd do that to your own son."

Greer had just said, "Mayhap. Why do you care? You've killed plenty of men over the years. You can't make me feel guilty."

"But they were laddies, Greer. One of them is your own son. Have you no conscience?"

Greer chuckled. "Apparently not. I might search for a

few more to add to their collection. This is more coin than we've had in years."

After hearing that, Cairstine had crept from her chair toward the staircase, but Greer must have heard her because he returned to the hall, grabbed her plait, and pulled her back. "You aren't going up there. You'll sit here, so when he returns, I still have you as a bargaining chip."

"Why don't we just leave?" Blair asked.

"And go where? We have nowhere to go, and there are Grants everywhere. Let them come after us, and we can send our men out to fight while we go out the back. If they're all focused here, then we can get away."

"He won't be back, Greer. I saw what your men did to him. He was nearly dead."

Greer chuckled. "Aye, they did do a nice job on him. I hope he *is* dead." He scowled as another thought crossed his mind. She had no idea what he was up to now. Greer had always been a bad man, but this moodiness was something new, and it worried her. It made him completely unpredictable.

"I thought you said you'd take me to Steenie," she whined, hoping to annoy him.

"I never claimed to be a man of my word, wench. I have no idea where he is." He moved over to a side table, took a jug, and filled a chipped goblet with ale.

"You truly sold our son?" she asked as he chugged down the ale. "How could you do such a thing, Greer? Even I didn't think you were so cold. Steenie loves you."

"Not cold. We need the coin. Everything from the previous shipment is gone. With the wealth we'll get from this one, we can finally make plans to leave, find a new place. We could go into hiding for a long while with this much coin. Selling Steenie was a smart move. It's always possible to get a new son in time; coin is not so reliable to come upon."

Cairstine fell into a chair, sickened by her choice to stay

behind. She was more helpless than she would have been had she left with Braden. He may not have known where Steenie was, but she believed with her whole heart that he would have searched all of Scotland for him.

For her. What had she done?

Of course, she didn't fully believe Greer would have let them go. Had she chosen the man her heart yearned for, he may have killed both of them.

Without warning, the front door burst open and two of Greer's guards stood in the entryway, both trying to catch their breath. "Guess who's back?" one of them said.

Could it be? Her heart leapt into her throat.

Greer peered over at her and said, "Stay here until I tell you to move." He turned toward his guards and sheathed his sword, which had been lying across a nearby table. "And how does he look?"

"He looks rough, chief. Don't know how the lad is still standing. They did a good job on him."

"What does he want this time?"

The guard looked at him strangely before he followed Greer out the door. "You. He wants you."

Blair came bolting out of the kitchens, yelping as he raced through the hall. "Greer. Wait for me." He glanced at Cairstine. "What happened?"

She shrugged, not wishing to speak to either of the brothers ever again. She also had no intention of following orders. As soon as she thought it was safe, she'd slip outside. Creeping over to the door, she opened it, giving herself just a small slit to view the courtyard. It didn't help. All the activity had moved toward the gate.

What had compelled Braden to come back? The man had actually kissed her, and the biggest surprise of all was that she had enjoyed it. Could he be returning for her?

Impossible. Her shoulders slumped because she recalled how she'd spit on the man. She hadn't wished to, but Greer had forced her into doing something she hadn't wanted, just as he always did. How she prayed Braden had been able to interpret her message and understood her motives.

Braden Grant was probably back because Greer had obviously stolen a Grant lad, Kennie or something like that. He was that noble, facing a group that had nearly killed him over the life of a wee laddie.

She had to admit that if she was around him more, she'd probably fall in love with him, if she knew what love was.

Love was elusive and always would be to her. She loved her son and had loved her family, but could she ever love a man who rutted on her? Probably not.

But she was as close to loving Braden as she'd been to loving any man. She loved his tenderness, his honesty, his demeanor, the way he held her, and the way he looked at her. In fact, thinking about him helped her make up her mind. She was going outside to watch everything, because if she could help Braden at all, she would. He'd tried to protect her more than once. Something caught her eye on a nearby table—a sharp dagger. She grabbed it, hid it, and headed out the door.

———◆———

BRADEN STOOD OUTSIDE THE GATES, his sword in his hand. Lamont's men had done some damage to his arm, but not his fighting arm. He couldn't wait to show the bastard his skills. He fought the desire to glance over his shoulder to see if his cousins had arrived. The last thing he wished to do was give them away, and he knew they'd stay back until he needed them.

A moment later, Greer Lamont came through the gates, looking as arrogant as ever. "They did a fine job on you, Grant. Have you not learned your lesson? I'm not sure they'll be so generous as to spare your life this time." he said with a grin.

Braden didn't answer, knowing he needed to draw him closer, close enough that he could catch the fool if he ran.

He said nothing, waiting for the arse to continue to shoot off taunts that didn't bother him. Uncle Alex's lesson had stayed with him. Never listen to the fool threatening you. Teach him the error of his ways by being the stronger man. Without moving his eyes, he noticed Gregor in a tree not far away. He knew Maggie and Gavin were also in position. Three guards followed Greer as his protection, and his brother Blair came barreling out through the gates, afraid he would miss something.

All was going exactly to plan.

He waited, though his urge to be impulsive nearly killed him, until just the right time. He'd hoped Cairstine would come out, but he didn't see her. He'd have to find her afterward. As soon as Greer was close enough, he flicked his left wrist—the signal he'd agreed upon with his cousins—and all hell broke loose.

Braden swung his sword over his head and ran straight at Greer, who barely managed to block what might have been a fatal blow.

One arrow caught the man to his right, a second arrow caught the guard to his left, and a third arrow caught the last guard. Perfect shots. Blair raced back into the keep, calling for all their guards to protect the castle.

A slew of guards flooded through the gates as Connor and Roddy joined the melee with the Grant guards, a welcome canvas of red plaids everywhere. The Grant war whoop echoed in Braden's ears as arrows continued to take Lamont men out.

Greer roared into attack mode, but Braden stayed calm as he went after the bastard who'd massacred the Muirs and raped Cairstine. They parried, moving several steps back toward the keep, close enough for Braden to notice Cairstine standing in the courtyard. She moved toward the gate and he yelled at her, "Stay inside, Cairstine." She froze in the gateway. "Step back. Archers." True, he'd wanted her safe, but he'd hoped she could get out ahead of the battle. Once the archers started shooting, it was safer for her inside the keep.

And less of a distraction for him. She understood him enough to move back to the courtyard.

He had to focus on Greer. Lamont's skills were not great, but Braden could tell he'd lost much of his own stamina in his battle with Lamont's guards. They'd weakened him considerably, or he'd have sliced Greer's throat twice over by now. Shocked to realize his vision was blurring, he forced himself to focus.

His only chance was to catch Greer off guard. If he failed, he'd probably take a blade in his own belly because he could feel his strength waning. He gave one last war whoop and swung at Greer from the right.

Greer blocked it with a roar.

Then from the left.

The arse blocked him again.

Then he brought his sword over his head and swung down as hard as he could. Their blades collided and rang out, but Greer held strong against him. Their faces were a hand's length apart as each tried to push his blade into the other.

"Weakening, Grant? You'll not be able to hold that sword for long. You're losing your stamina. After what my men took out of you, you'll be a dead man within minutes."

"I warned you, Lamont. I told you that you'd pay for hurting Cairstine. That I'd kill you with my own hands."

Greer laughed. "And who's the stronger one now?" The cords in his neck stood out, evidence of how hard he worked to hold Braden off.

Braden gritted his teeth, pulling everything he could from deep in his gut. "Don't look around much or you'll see how fast your men are going down. Grant warriors and archers have taken out half of them already." He saw a glimpse of uncertainty in Greer's gaze as his eyes flitted to the side and back again. Now he had the bastard.

Braden had to end this soon. When he pulled from his gut to push harder, to his surprise, Greer came up with a surge of power and shoved him back. The force made him turn his back to Lamont. Greer was ready to take advantage of it, but then the arrogant bastard made a big mistake. Before he swung his sword down, aiming to slice Braden in two, he paused for long enough to shoot him a haughty grin.

A fatal mistake, according to Braden's sire and uncles. The smile weakened him and left him vulnerable.

Braden spun in the opposite direction, bringing his sword in a wide arc from the side, catching Greer by surprise. He had been so quick to celebrate his victory, he hadn't anticipated Braden's move at all.

Greer's sword was just starting to drop in what he thought would be his final blow when Braden's sword struck him from the side, nearly cleaving him in two across his waist.

The shock registered in his eyes for a split second, long enough for Braden to lift his foot and kick him backward, forcing him to drop his sword.

Before he took his last breath, Greer managed to spit out another vile word, "Bastard…"

Braden moved over the swine, placed his foot on his chest and spit on him. "That's for Cairstine and all of Clan Muir."

Braden wiped the sweat from his brow before he turned around, pleased to see there were only two or three Lamont men still fighting, but they were quickly taken out by Grant warriors.

When the last man was struck down, a round of cheers echoed around him as he scanned the area for another attacker. "Any of our men hurt?"

Roddy and Connor both shook their heads as they walked through the battlefield checking. "Only a couple of small slices." The archers dropped out of the trees with a cheer. Suddenly, out of the corner of his eye, he caught another movement.

Cairstine. She flew across the courtyard and out through the gates in a dead run, headed straight for him, then jumped into his arms and wrapped her arms around his neck. She let out a sob but then cupped his face and kissed him, another round of cheers ringing out around them.

When she ended the kiss, she whispered, "You've brought vengeance to my clan, Braden Grant. I will thank you well enough in time but there's another life that still needs saving. Please, help me find Steenie?"

CHAPTER SIXTEEN

———◆———

A S BRADEN SET CAIRSTINE'S FEET back down
on the ground, he kissed her forehead. Yet she knew
something was not right.

"Braden? You don't look well." She could feel the slight
tremor in his legs.

Connor came up to him first. "I've seen that expression before. Sit on that log. Roddy, go inside and find him
something to drink. Here's an oatcake." He handed it to
him, but Braden continued to stare at him, running his
hand up and down Cairstine's back.

Maggie said, "Braden, you fought a hell of a fight, as we
all did, but you had already been through hell. You need to
sit down before you collapse. We'll find you something to
eat and drink."

"I'll go," Cairstine said. "I know where the food is kept."

Braden held onto her wrist lightly. "Take someone with
you. Roddy, go with her, please. Blair ran inside. Who
knows if he's still lurking around in there."

Roddy motioned to three guards to follow him inside.
Cairstine stayed outside the door until they waved her in.

"He's not here." Roddy said as she stepped into the great
hall. "No one's here. I found a jug of ale and some goblets.
Any cheese or bread you can find?"

"Aye," she ran into the kitchens and gathered a few
things for Braden and the others.

They carried the repast outside, and once they were settled under a shady tree, Braden introduced her to his cousins. "Tell us what you know, Cairstine. I could tell you had more information than we do."

She kneaded her hands in her lap and explained everything she knew. The last few comments she said were the most frightening, but she had to tell them. "When I was locked up in the cellars, I heard some strange noises coming from down the passageway."

Maggie asked, "Did you ever determine the source?"

She nodded. "Bairns. I'm certain they were keeping bairns there. I heard wee lassies crying. Hilda, my maid, was tending them, I'm certain of it. I asked her about it, and she said there were things she had to do that she hated, and it was better if I didn't know."

Will nodded. "This has to be the source of the Firth of Clyde channel. It explains how the Lamonts have survived here. I see few fields; no tanner, weaver, or blacksmith."

"All I can tell you is the brothers often argued about coin, and they went to market frequently to buy what we needed. We had a cook, and they hunted often, but other goods were bought from the outside."

Will paced behind Braden. "They were not self-sustaining. They needed coin. I suspect they could be one of the major suppliers to the Channel."

"Of bairns?" Cairstine asked, afraid to hear the answer. Could this have been going on for some time without her knowing it? "Where do they get them?"

Maggie said, "They kidnap them or find families with too many mouths to feed. Convince a sire to sell one or two of their daughters off. 'Tis how it went with my sister and me, though we were never in the Channel."

"I've learned more than I care to know about it today."

"I'm sorry, Cairstine," Will said. "We're here to help you and your lad. Can you lead me to the place they were kept, see if there's any evidence to help us find them?"

"Aye. Follow me."

Braden tried to get up. Will placed his hand on his shoulder and said, "You're staying here with Connor. Roddy, Maggie, and I will go."

"I should come."

"Braden," Will said, using a tone that told her he wouldn't brook any argument. "We're leaving in ten minutes. If you don't save your strength, you'll never make it the distance. In fact, Cairstine will ride with you so you don't fall off your horse. Sit and eat and gather your strength, or we'll leave you behind. I cannot afford to have you slow us down."

The thought of leaving him behind, even for a short while, horrified her. Cairstine said, "Sit, Braden. Please?" She cupped his cheek and kissed him. "I care not to lose you. We've only just found each other."

He nodded and settled in a spot where he could lean against the tree, waving at Roddy to move on.

Cairstine looked back at him once before she led them into the keep. The smile he summoned for her was surely the sweetest she'd ever seen. Holding that feeling with her, letting it warm her, she led the way into the cellars. "I'm not sure which chamber, but 'twas down near the end."

They searched from door to door, and finally Maggie said, "Here."

Once they were inside, no one spoke. The floor was scattered with small plaids, a few pallets, and fabric animals. The chamber was quite cold. "Three bairns?" Roddy asked.

Maggie picked up one of the fabric dogs. "Nay, I'm sure there were more. They can pack several of them onto a pallet. There were six or eight."

"How can you be so sure?" Will asked, walking over to wrap his arm around her shoulder.

"I don't know how I know, but I can feel it." She glanced at Will, her eyes saddened. "There were at least six, and all of them were lassies." She swiped a tear away and then turned toward the door.

Cairstine said, "With Steenie and Kenzie, they could have up to ten bairns."

"We have to hurry to catch up with Loki."

———◆———

HILDA HUGGED HIM AND THEN pushed him away. "I did not want you to see me, lad. But why are you here, Steenie? You should not be. Your poor mother." Her face looked as if she were about to cry.

"Don't cry, Hilda. I ran away again. I tried to get to the Grants and Loki found me and this is his son Kenzie and he helped me come save my mama because they were not going to come until morning and I feared for her too much…"

"Hold, lad. Calm down. It does not matter now." She turned around to look at Kenzie.

"You were going to hit me with that?" She took the piece of wood out of his hand and threw it outside the door.

"Nay, 'twas for the mean man. We must escape."

"Hilda, will you help us?" Kenzie asked.

Tears filled her eyes and she swiped them away. "I hate this, whatever it is they do with these bairns. 'Tis not right."

One of the older girls came over. "Where are they taking us?"

Hilda sighed. "I really do not know. We take you to the loch and put you on a boat that travels down to the firth. This is the first time we've had such wee ones. I don't like it. They told me they'll sell you to women who don't have bairns of their own. If it were the truth, I could be happy for you, but when I look at the men you'll travel with?" She never finished her sentence, instead shaking her head and dotting her eyes with a linen square to soak up her tears. "This is out of my control, but I must do something.

I cannot help them any longer."

"Then take us out of here." Steenie tugged on her skirts while he pleaded. "Please."

"Careful, lad. 'Tis not that easy." She sighed and dried her tears. "Give me a moment to think." After a few seconds of silence, she turned to Kenzie. "What clan do you belong to?"

"Clan Grant."

She let out a low whistle. "Then perhaps we have a chance."

Steenie tugged on Hilda's hand. "Aye, the Grants are the biggest and strongest ever. They'll save us. Do you not agree, Kenzie?"

"Aye, my papa will come. These men can't get away with this."

"The Grants must hurry." Steenie hopped from one foot to the other while they waited. Kenzie kept signaling for him to relax, but he couldn't. He wouldn't be able to relax until he got away. Until they all did.

"Here's what I think," Hilda said. "We're not to the loch yet. When we get there, there are two buildings in a clearing. One building is near the end of the loch and the other is tucked in behind it. I've slept there before. Mayhap I can sneak some of you away into the back building and they'll not notice. Keep you hidden and not put you on the boat."

"Who would you choose?" Kenzie asked.

The eldest lass said, "The bairns shouldn't be forced to go. What if they...?"

"What if they what?" Steenie asked.

"Never mind, Steenie, but she's right," Hilda said. "I must save the wee lassies first, and then you'll be next."

"But if Loki Grant comes, he'll save us all," Steenie pointed out.

"Aye," Kenzie said. "If he can find us, he'll save us all. But what if they don't find us?"

Steenie tugged on Kenzie's plaid, staring up at his new

friend. "You must leave, Kenzie. 'Tis all my fault you're here."

"I've been saved once, so I know how it feels." Kenzie patted his shoulder. "And I'm older. She's right. The youngest must be saved first. Papa would say to save the lassies. We're lads, Steenie. We must go last."

"Aye," Steenie said, with a wee bit of a pout. "Save the lassies first. I'll stay with Kenzie so Hilda can go with them." He pointed to the bigger lass next to him. "Otherwise, where will they go alone? They'll need someone to look after them."

"Are you sure, Steenie?" Hilda asked.

"Aye, 'tis what a Grant warrior would do. And if I'm ever freed, I'll come back to be a Grant warrior, the fiercest of them all!"

CHAPTER SEVENTEEN

———————

B RADEN MOUNTED AND HAD WILL lift Cairstine up in front of him. Once he had her settled, Braden said, "My thanks, Will. You were right. I needed to close my eyes for a moment. I believe I slept for ten minutes while you were inside, and I feel much better. I'm ready now."

"Good. Let's get away to the loch to meet Loki and save the bairns."

"I hope we don't find Blair there," Cairstine said.

"Blair Lamont will likely disappear for some time now, especially once he finds out his brother is dead. He's lost too many men to defend the Muir Castle. If you want to take Muir Castle back, talk to Uncle Alex, Braden. I don't think you'll have any difficulty."

"How long will it take to get to the loch, Will?" Cairstine asked.

"Probably two hours. 'Tis not far, but the path will be treacherous at times because of the mountains." Will patted the horse and headed toward his own.

As soon as Will mounted, Braden fell in behind him. They were to ride in the middle of the group in case Braden took sick along the way. The path would be narrow at times, but not to begin with.

He hadn't even thought about Muir Castle, but now that the idea had been mentioned, he tried to imagine what it would be like to live there with Cairstine and the lad, so close to his family.

Once they were on their way, Cairstine turned toward him. "Braden, may I ask you something?"

"Of course." He had no idea what she wished to discuss, but they had a long trip ahead of them. Talking was probably what they needed to do most. His feelings were in such a jumble at the moment.

"I know we've only just met, but you kissed me and it was the first kiss I've ever received from a man that made me feel special," she paused as if considering her words carefully. "I'm naïve about lads and love. But I wonder if that kiss also meant something to you?"

"Of course, it did. I would not have kissed you had I not been interested in you. Your strength, your resilience, both impress me and you're a beautiful woman. I'd hoped mayhap we'd get to know each other better once this is over. That is, if 'tis what you want, too. You'll never be forced into another man's company again, Cairstine—not by me or anyone else—from now on."

She spun around to look at him, gazing into his eyes. "Aye. I would like that verra much. In fact, I feel 'tis important for me to warn you of something. I fear I may tell you I'm in love with you before you are ready to hear it. Just understand what my life has been."

He started to speak, but she stopped him, and a part of him was glad because he wasn't ready to tell her he loved her, simply because he was unsure. Now that she was close to him, he had his arm around her waist, and it pleased him to hold her close. But he didn't know her well enough to talk about love.

Or did he? She'd affected him more than any other lass. That had to mean something. He couldn't deny that when Cairstine had spit on him, it had felt like he'd been bludgeoned—straight to the middle of his chest. He couldn't explain it exactly, but seeing her strength, her comportment through all the situations the Lamonts put her through…his feelings had blossomed in that moment into something different and unexpected. His admiration for her had grown four-fold in that one instance. It was as though he'd been struck soundly in the head.

Was that love?

He'd heard lasses talk about love before, but he hadn't heard much from lads. Men didn't discuss emotions. What he did remember is that his sire had said it happened as soon as he'd stood near his mother. He'd known then she was the one.

Had that happened to him on Drummond land? Had it progressed to something even stronger when they'd stood together in front of Greer Lamont?

What if she told him she was going to leave after this in search of other family members far away?

He had to admit that thought would not sit well with him. He'd probably follow her.

"Please allow me to say what is on my mind before you speak."

"Go ahead. I'm listening," he whispered with a squeeze to her waist, his mind more muddled than ever.

"My mama used to talk to me about lads when I was young. If she were riding next to us, she would tell me that I don't know you well enough to love you. That I mentioned love to the first lad who was nice to me, that Greer and Blair were so cruel in comparison, for so long, it was normal that I would fall in love with the first kind lad I met."

He could tell by the tone of her voice that she fought tears. The memories of the family she'd lost were still so painful to her.

"But I would tell her that you are exactly like the man she said I would love one day. She told me that she hoped my future husband and I would share all the wonderful things she'd shared with Papa. I asked her how I would know…" She paused for a second to wipe her tears. "She told me that a good husband would protect me. He would be kind and gentle. He'd never raise a hand to me, and he'd be considerate of my feelings, too. He'd share his thoughts with me and accept me as his partner. She told me something else that I never understood until now, that the man I loved would make my belly flutter. 'Tis exactly how I feel when I'm around you. So I would tell Mama—" she glanced off to the side as if imagining her mother there, "—that you are all those things. That mayhap I already love you. That you are kind and considerate, and perhaps I shouldn't have told you how I feel, but I don't think my feelings will change."

"Good. I'm glad," he said, squeezing her waist slightly. She reached down and squeezed back.

"Forgive me. Mama said men do not like to talk about feelings and love, that I would know if a relationship was right in other ways. And I know she was right. 'Tis all I wished to say." She leaned back against him as if she'd lifted the weight of a warhorse from her shoulders.

Braden struggled with what to say because she was correct about one thing. He didn't like to talk about feelings, yet he owed her something. That wasn't true. He *wished* to tell her something. But he did not understand the concept of love. True, he loved his parents and so many of the members of his clan, but this was different.

How would he know when it was love?

He needed time to settle his thoughts, so he just told her what was on his mind. "These last few days have been a whirlwind, and we're still in the midst of it. We will have plenty of time to see exactly how we feel about each other. I know I've been attracted to you since the first time I laid eyes on you at Drummond Castle, and I'm verra pleased to have you tucked against me on this horse and away from Greer Lamont. I'm not sure if I love you, I've never been in love before, but I'd like to find out. Is that enough for now?"

She whirled her head back to face him, a wide grin on her face. "Aye," she said with a nod. "I can ask for naught more than that, Braden Grant. Many thanks to you for all you've done for me." She kissed him, a quick kiss because they were on the horse, but it was enough for now.

And the only thought that echoed through his mind was that he wanted more than that kiss. He wanted everything. He wanted her heart, and he'd do whatever he could to make her happy.

His sire's words echoed in his mind, the words about a lass taking over his thoughts.

He was in love with Cairstine Muir. A broad smile broke out across his face at that thought, but he was glad she didn't see it. There were more pressing matters at the moment.

First, they had to find Steenie.

———————◆———————

IT HAD BEEN TERRIBLY DIFFICULT for Steenie to mind his tongue with the men who'd come to put them in a cart and carry them through the mountains toward the loch. The one trail had been so treacherous that the wee bairns had cried for their mamas over and over again, and the four men traveling with them had not been kind. They'd cussed at them so much that Steenie had wished to hit each of them with his fist. He wanted his arms to be like tree trunks like Robbie and Braden Grant's so he could punch them and make them stop being so mean.

He flexed his muscles to check them out, wondering how he could get them to be so big.

"You have to work in the Grant lists, Steenie," Kenzie whispered.

"Huh?"

"I saw you looking at your muscles. You want them big like the Grants, do you not?"

Steenie nodded, his face lighting up. "Aye, how can I get them that big?"

"You have to work in the lists. They work there every day."

"Can I when we get out? I'll get mine to be bigger." He flexed his one arm to demonstrate to Kenzie how big his was already.

Kenzie said with a grin, "When you're a wee bit older, mayhap."

"I'll practice every day." He was sure he could get his arms to be bigger.

Before he knew it, they'd made it through and were drawing near the loch.

When they could see the loch ahead, Kenzie leaned over to whisper to Steenie. "If you see any hawks or falcons overhead, especially more than one, 'tis a good sign."

"Why?" Steenie whispered.

"Because my cousin married the Wild Falconer and Uncle Alex sent for them, though 'tis unlikely they're here yet. But Papa says they do amazing things. Have you not heard about him?"

Steenie shook his head, his eyes widening. "What does he do?"

"He can send his birds down to attack mean people. They've done it before and 'tis spectacular. If you see them, it means my cousins are here."

"You two lads keep quiet back there. I shoulda split you two up." The lead man had a long scruffy beard that hit his chest.

"Scruffy…" Steenie whispered. Then he looked at Kenzie and giggled. That was one of the activities that had helped them make it through the night—giving names to all of their captors. Scruffy, Blackteeth, Stubby—because he'd lost two fingers—and Smelly.

He peeked at the two lassies in the cart with them. They were sisters, and one had her head in her sister's lap while she sucked her thumb. "Why does she suck her thumb still? I don't."

"Because she watched her mother die not long ago. She's sucked it ever since," the girl named Edith said bluntly. She turned her head away from Steenie, and he wondered if she was mad he'd asked such a direct question.

"What's her name?" he asked, hoping to get her to talk to him again. He would feel horrible if he lost his mother, especially if something happened to her in front of him and he wasn't able to stop it.

"Eva."

"How old is she?"

"She's eight summers."

"How did you get here?"

"Two of these men came and killed our mother, then stole us from my aunt. We were living with her." She wiped the tears that formed in the corners of her eyes. "Do you know where they're taking us?"

"Nay, but do not worry," Kenzie said. "My sire will save us. Watch for the falcons and slingers."

"Slingers?" she whispered.

"Aye. My sire is the best. He slings small rocks at bad men."

A bold voice shouted back at them from the front. "I said keep quiet. All of you."

Kenzie held his finger up to his lips. Steenie scowled, but there was naught they could do but listen. Both lads tipped their heads back, and Steenie hoped he'd see a bunch of wild falcons.

He wished to meet the Wild Falconer. Maybe someday he could *be* a Wild Falconer.

There weren't any falcons in eyesight, so Steenie shifted his gaze to the path ahead of them, just then realizing he could see the loch. He pointed his finger toward the water, and Kenzie glanced over his shoulder to follow. When they came down the hill, there was a large clearing on one side of the loch with a couple of small huts near one end. He could see clear across to the other side because it was so big.

He didn't like the boat at the edge. Two men were stacking crates around the lip of the loch while three men worked on the boat, getting water, sweeping the boat out, spitting over the edge.

He watched the man spit over and over again. Someday he'd be able to spit that far. He decided to practice a bit, so he spat over the side of the cart to see how far it would go. He did this for a while until Kenzie poked him in his back.

He peered over his shoulder at Kenzie, who pointed up to the sky. He was careful to make sure no one else saw what he was doing, so Steenie guessed it was important. He tipped his head up toward the gray sky, but he didn't see anything at first. A moment later, two big birds soared above them, sweeping lower and lower.

He couldn't help but clap his hands.

"What the hell is with the birds? They've been following us for the last quarter hour," Stubby yelled.

Scruffy shouted back at him. "Who cares? They're just birds, you daft arse." Then he spat to the side of his horse.

Steenie giggled and whispered, "Daft arse." Then he spat over the side, pleased that it was farther than his previous marks.

Blackteeth pulled the first cart full of girls, also carrying Hilda, into the clearing, waving to the men aboard the boat. Then he cursed and slapped the back of his head. Spinning around on his horse, he stared at Scruffy who was mounted behind him.

"What the hell? Why are you throwing stones at me?"

Kenzie pulled on Steenie's tunic, wide-eyed. He whispered, "My sire. He's here!"

Scruffy said, "I didn't throw naught at you, but I will if you don't keep moving."

The two men who'd ridden by themselves climbed

down and moved over to the cart in front, lifting the lassies out one by one and pushing them toward the boat. One of the men roared as his head was jerked backward. "Who did that?" he shouted, his hand flying up to his forehead.

Steenie watched as Kenzie pulled out his own slinger, stuck a rock in it and sent it flying at the man who'd been in the first cart, hitting him in the back of the head. "I grabbed the stones when we got into the cart when the men weren't looking," he explained with a whisper.

Blackteeth turned on Scruffy and shouted, "You bastard. 'Tis the second time you've hit me. Come over here and try it. I'll kick your arse."

Scruffy got hit in the back of his head next. "I didn't do naught," he said, "but somebody just hit me."

The other cart had emptied, but Kenzie, Steenie, Edith, and Eva were still in their cart when the falcons dipped down from the sky again, soaring over the entire group of them.

"Kenzie, look. 'Tis the falcons again just like you said," Steenie whispered.

Their captors, nine in all—the four who'd brought them here and the five near the boat—started jabbering and shouting. Hilda must have sensed an opportunity, for she sent the girls running toward the huts at the end, but they were so confused, they ran in different directions.

All of a sudden, three horses carrying men with red plaids charged out of the woods. Kenzie grabbed Eva out of Edith's arms and said, "Run!"

Steenie hopped out of the cart and ran for the trees as fast as his wee legs could carry him. He knew those plaids. The Grants had come.

CHAPTER EIGHTEEN

M AGGIE HAD LED BRADEN AND the others down a rarely used path to the loch. He couldn't help but smile when he noticed Loki ahead of him, his slinger in hand. The others were gathered behind him. His brother was sheer magic with his slinger, able to catapult small rocks long distances with dead aim. He'd been doing it since he was young and living alone behind an inn.

Cairstine started to speak, but he squeezed her hip and covered her mouth. He pointed down to the loch, where he could just barely see the boat through the trees. It looked like there were several bairns in the clearing.

He heard Cairstine gasp.

"We found him. 'Tis what's important," he reminded her with a whisper. "And now we'll get him to safety." She spun around and nodded, her lips sealed.

They all took their places, not needing to converse with each other because they had planned their roles in advance. Gavin, Will, and Gregor would find perches where they could back the ground crew up with arrows, while Loki, Connor, and Roddy would use their swords, and Braden and Maggie would go scoop up the bairns, the archers protecting them. Usually Braden preferred sword-to-sword combat, but he was grateful Maggie had suggested this change. His body could only endure so much.

"What about Loki's group?" Braden had asked before

they set out.

Maggie had snorted, quite like a man, and said, "Loki planned to leave his guards at the top of the hill to search for any other men in the area before he joined us. He and Connor and Roddy are probably the best swordsmen in the Highlands. They don't need any instructions. With our three swordsmen and three archers, we can easily take on nine men."

Cairstine gave him a questioning look and said, "Nine to six?"

Braden grinned. "You've not seen all the Grants fight before, so I'll ignore that question. Do not worry about it. I'll bring the bairns to you, all of them. Can you handle it?"

She nodded. "Aye, absolutely."

Loki had worked his magic on the men near the boats, who had begun to argue and grab the backs of their heads. Braden moved close to Maggie and helped Cairstine dismount. "I'm leaving you behind in this small group of trees," he said to her, stroking her back. "You'll be safe. Maggie and I will stay on our horses, the others will fight on foot. When we grab the bairns, we'll bring them back to you. Just keep them hidden and safe until this is over."

She nodded, wringing her hands as she watched the activity by the loch. He understood how difficult it was for her to stay put and not go chasing after Steenie.

His cousins let their famous Grant war whoop loose, and chaos descended as they dismounted and went after the four bastards who'd smuggled the children. All of them were now on foot. He glanced at Cairstine one more time, the trust and hope in her gaze humbling him, then flicked the reins of his horse and flew into the middle of the clearing. The first thing he noticed was a wee lassie running in circles, so he headed straight for her, but she was too low to the ground for him to reach her. Then he saw Kenzie running toward him with a lass in his arms. "Here," he yelled. "Hand the lassie up to me."

Kenzie helped both lassies get settled on the horse.

"This way," Braden said to him. "Run on this side of my horse so the archers won't catch you." He turned his horse back toward the trees while Kenzie raced along next to him. Once he was out of range, he handed the two lassies to Cairstine and spoke to Kenzie. "Help her, lad. Maggie is bringing more." Then he turned back and headed toward the loch again once he noticed an older woman running with more bairns around her.

He saw Steenie at the same time Cairstine's scream carried to him. A man was running behind the lad, his sword arched over his head.

"Circle, Braden!" Gavin's instructions gave him exactly the information he needed, telling him how to approach and leave a shot for the archer.

He headed toward Steenie, who'd finally noticed him, and yelled, "Arms up, Steenie." Fortunately, the wee laddie understood him. He stuck both hands into the air and Braden leaned over and grabbed him by the waist. He feared he was going to lose him, but he said, "Grab my neck, Steenie." Then he circled around the attacker while Steenie grappled for balance on the horse. A second later an arrow sluiced through the air and caught the fool now in front of them square in the neck.

Steenie clutched him so tightly he had to say, "Let go, lad. I need to breathe." The look of relief on the lad's face released a knot of tension in his chest. The wee laddie was away from the kidnappers, and he'd soon be safe with his mama. Aside from Steenie loosening his grip, Braden could breathe again knowing that he'd fulfilled his promises to Cairstine. He'd show her he was a man of his word time and time again, starting with his latest vow to get to know her better once this war was over.

Braden headed to the trees and dropped Steenie into Cairstine's waiting arms.

"Mama! You're safe," Steenie said as she grabbed him and hugged him tight.

Braden's chest puffed out as he watched the two together. Cairstine glanced his way, such gratitude in her eyes that he was humbled.

But he couldn't wait any longer, so he swung back around. They really had no idea how many bairns were there. The number of enemies still swinging their swords was down from nine to five, though two had decided to give up and fled back to their boat.

Braden saw Maggie grab one of the small lassies, but he noticed one of the older ones was spinning around in a panic of confusion, gripping a young girl in her arms. It was obvious she didn't know where to run or who to trust. He shouted, "Hand her to me." The girl, crying furiously, held the wee lass up so Braden could grab her. Then he slowed, "Give me your hand and you can climb on behind me."

The lass stopped crying and let out a piercing scream unlike anything he'd ever heard before. Braden had no idea how to calm her. Then Cairstine's voice carried across the distance to him and the girl. "Edith, trust him."

Hell, but Cairstine knew the lass?

Edith must have recognized Cairstine, too, because she offered her hand to Braden and he tugged her up high enough that she could slide her leg over the horse behind him. Once she was steady, he led his horse away from the few battling men and over to the trees.

Once he set her feet on the ground, Edith, still in a panic, screamed, "Eva, where are you?"

Cairstine stepped out and said, "Here, Edith. She must be here." She pointed to the three lassies behind her, all of them now sobbing.

Edith shot over to the group, picking up her sister and holding her tight, sobbing uncontrollably. Then she turned to Cairstine and looked at her, but there was no recognition in her eyes.

"Edith," she said, "I'm Cairstine…your cousin."

———◆———

CAIRSTINE STEPPED CLOSER. ALL THE bairns who'd been brought to her were safely hidden amidst the trees, including Steenie and Kenzie, so she moved closer to speak to the poor girl. Could it truly be her? "You are Edith, are you not? Edith of the Muirs? It must be you. I'll never forget your sire teaching us all to scream like that if we were ever in trouble." She patted her shoulder and said, "You did it perfectly. Your sire would be proud."

Edith nodded, still holding Eva tight against her. She looked pale and shaky, as though she were about to drop.

Cairstine spoke gently to her. "Is this your wee sister, Eva? I remember her as a babe. I'm your cousin. Your mother was my sire's sister. Papa was laird of the Muirs." She reached up to brush a few stray hairs back from Edith's face. "I thought you'd all died in the attack six years ago."

"Cairstine? Truly?" Her voice came out in a tremulous tone, and her hands shook.

"Aye, 'tis me. Trust these men. Where have you been? I didn't know you survived. Where is your mother?"

Edith hugged Cairstine and then stepped back to lean against a tree. Eva still clutched her sister, but her gaze followed Cairstine. "When the men came for us a sennight ago, they killed Mama. Mama, Eva, and I were visiting Aunt Fina when the attack on the castle happened many years ago. The three of us have lived with her ever since, but these kidnappers came when Aunt Fina was out hunting. 'Twas just Mama and the two of us, and she couldn't fight them off." Her shoulders slumped before she lifted her gaze back to Cairstine. "I did not know you survived that day, Cairstine. We thought everyone had perished but the three of us. Mama and Aunt Fina went back several times over the next year searching for anyone, especially Papa, but never found any survivors. Our clanmates who were away and had escaped the brutality told Aunt Fina to keep her distance because the attackers were monsters. We were afraid. But no matter how much room we put between us and Muir Castle, and how careful we have been, this happened."

"Nearly everyone perished during the attack. I was the only one taken captive. Corc was allowed to stay on." She pulled Steenie away from Kenzie and said, "This is my son, Steafan. I call him Steenie. Steenie, these two are your cousins, Edith and Eva." Turning back to the lasses, she smiled and gestured to Braden, "And this is Braden Grant. His cousins are the ones who saved you."

Eva took her thumb out of her mouth and smiled at Cairstine. "May we go home with you?"

Cairstine didn't know what to tell her, so she simply nodded. She wished to keep the lasses calm.

Of course, she had no idea where she and Steenie would be living.

Braden kissed her forehead and said, "Do not worry. We'll go back to Clan Grant to feed everyone. We don't need to decide everything just yet." He said to Edith, "We have hundreds of guards to protect you."

Edith whispered, "Hundreds? Those men, the ones that killed Mama, they're not all here. Please protect us?"

"We will. There are at least fifty Grant warriors at the top of the ravine, and my guess is another hundred are on their way. Clan Grant has over five hundred warriors. We'll put an end to this atrocity and send someone for your Aunt Fina, if you like."

Edith's eyes misted and she kissed her sister's forehead. "Eva, you see. They'll protect us from those nasty men."

He tugged Cairstine close, but soon someone whistled. It was an alert Braden recognized, for he helped her up and then took Steenie by the hand. As he led them over to his cousins, Steenie's wee friend, Kenzie, bolted past them to stand at the side of a tall man—his sire, no doubt. The cousins met in a circle, and Braden quickly introduced her and Steenie to everyone they had not yet met. She still didn't understand all that had transpired. Where had that boat been headed?

Maggie said, "Well done, we have a better understanding of how this organization works, but we still don't know who runs it. Mayhap when we return and get to talk to everyone, we'll be able to find out more."

Braden tugged on her hand. "I'll explain everything later."

She nodded, unsure if she could handle all that information at the moment. Looking at the wee lassies still sitting near the trees, she couldn't imagine what they'd all been through.

The one called Loki said, "Well, there are nine less rat bastards. 'Tis something. *This* sale is not taking place. Wherever they were headed, someone will have a long wait."

Steenie leaned against his mother and giggled with his hand over his mouth from Loki's comment.

"I was so scared." Kenzie wrapped his arms around his sire's waist. "But I knew you'd come, Papa."

"Did either of you hear any names?" Will asked. "Do you know who the leader was?"

Kenzie said, "Nay." Then he scowled, stepping back to search the area as though he'd forgotten something. "Where did she go, Steenie?"

Steenie hopped in place three times. "I forgot Hilda. Where is she? Mama, Hilda was with us. Hilda?" He ran toward the trees opposite them, but before he could disappear from sight a woman stepped out from behind the tree cover, a fearful expression on her face. Maggie and Will approached her along with Kenzie.

Will asked, "Are you a part of this group?"

Hilda broke into tears. "Only because they forced me to care for the bairns. I didn't want to do it. Blair and Greer wouldn't take no for an answer, and I had been forced into a life at Muir Castle. Sad life as 'twas. I couldn't leave Cairstine and Steenie alone to the men."

"Greer will not be in charge of Muir Castle any longer," Will said. "Blair has disappeared. He'll not bother you for a while. I'm sure he's in hiding. Are you kin to them?"

"Nay. They kidnapped me from a cottage five winters ago. Killed my husband and told me I needed to help a woman who was carrying. I've been with them ever since. I've always hated both of them."

Cairstine wrapped her arms around Hilda, showing her allegiance to her, and nodded to indicate the woman was telling the truth. "She was as much a prisoner as I was."

Maggie moved closer to her and placed her hand on the woman's shoulder. "You're welcome to travel to Grant land with us. In fact, I would appreciate it if you would be willing to answer some questions. For now, I think we should get away from this area. Do you know of anyone else who was supposed to be here?"

Hilda shook her head.

Maggie said, "Will, let's search the huts. Connor, you check the boat." A group moved to the end to the buildings while Connor and Roddy climbed onto the boat to search it for any clues.

Cairstine squeezed Hilda one last time and stepped back. "What about Corc? Did he accompany the guards?"

"Aye," Loki said, "but we left him atop the hill with the guards. We'll bring him back to Clan Grant. Maggie said there's naught left at Muir Castle but dead bodies."

Maggie turned to the group and said, "Let's head back to Clan Grant. They can feed all of us, then we'll see what we can learn from the bairns. Some of them may have homes. I'm not convinced no one else will come this way. 'Tis best to be safe."

Maggie moved over to the lassies still in the trees, speaking first with the older lasses before helping them up.

Cairstine and Hilda followed her, each picking up a bairn to console her.

Loki said, "We'll send guards out to see how many of Lamont's men may have survived."

Maggie assigned a bairn to each horseman. Steenie said, "Who can I ride with? You, Mama?"

Before she could answer, Braden whispered in his ear, "I'd like to take you back to your castle to pick up a few things for you and your son. I don't think it would be wise to take Steenie there."

The thought hadn't even occurred to Cairstine, but he was right, of course. She wasn't sure what had become of the bodies they'd left behind. The last thing she wanted was for her son to see more bloodshed, particularly since his father was among the fallen. Wicked or not, Greer had been her boy's sire.

When she nodded and squeezed his hand, he made the suggestion to Maggie.

"Wise plan and I agree," Maggie said. "He's welcome to ride with Will."

Braden asked, "Would you like to ride with Will, the Wild Falconer?"

"Aye," Steenie shouted. "May I?" It made Cairstine grin to see him so happy. Besides, these were men he could look up to—men who would not take advantage of either of them.

Steenie raced over to Will's horse, staring up at him, his exuberance showing. "Can I see the falcons? We watched them soar through the air and we knew you'd come to save us!"

Just to show off a little, Will held his arm up and the peregrine landed, his wings spread wide before tucking them in. Steenie jumped up and down with excitement, his enthusiasm spreading to the others.

"Steenie. Come say goodbye," Cairstine said, reaching for him. She wanted to hold him one more time to assure herself he was safe. "We'll arrive at Clan Grant a few hours after you. Will you be all right with Kenzie and Will?"

Steenie nodded and tried to jump on the horse, but Will kept him down. "Always be good to your mother. Say goodbye to your mama first." He set the falcon off into the air again.

Steenie charged at her, hugged her quick, and said, "Bye, Mama. See you soon. I'm a Wee Wild Falconer now." He hurried back, but then stopped. He swiveled around to look at her and said, "Mama, I don't think we'll see Papa again." He paused to stare at his feet, his finger resting on his lip. "I heard one of the bad men say Papa was a dead man. They said he'd gotten into too much trouble this time. But I don't mind if it means he won't hit either one of us anymore. And he cannot lock you up now."

Dead silence fell on the group. All activity stopped at Steenie's comment.

She rushed over to her son, hugged him, then kissed his forehead. "Papa will not be hitting either one of us ever again. We'll talk later. Does that suit you?" After all he'd been through, she wasn't ready to discuss the realities of death with him quite yet. That time would come soon enough. For the journey home, he could be the Wee Wild Falconer. He deserved every bit of happiness he could get.

"Aye," Steenie called over his shoulder as he ran to Will's horse. Within moments, he was already peppering Will with more questions about the falcons.

Cairstine couldn't help but smile. How she adored her son.

She glanced at Braden and realized something.

The worst was over. Greer was gone forever, and Steenie was hale.

It was time to start living her life the way *she* chose.

CHAPTER NINETEEN

B RADEN PRAYED THERE WOULDN'T BE anyone at Muir Castle, even reivers. He was exhausted and wasn't ready to swing his sword again quite yet. He ached in so many places, he struggled to ignore all the pain.

The biggest ache presently was in his groin. Considering all the pain he still suffered, he'd assumed he wouldn't have any reaction to Cairstine being so close to him.

He'd been wrong. Her soft bottom rubbed against him most of the trip, and as soon as they'd split from that group a short time ago, his erection had commanded his attention.

Cairstine wasn't a naïve lass either. At one point, she'd glanced over her shoulder at him and said, "I'm sorry. Would you like me to ride behind you?"

He'd chuckled and said, "Nay. I like you where you are. It gives me an ache that helps me forget the rest of my pain."

There was one thing he had to tell her that might relax his need, so he plunged ahead. "Cairstine, I doubt you'll find Greer's body. I don't know what you'd hoped for, but I'd guess that my uncle sent more men and had them bury the dead. He often sends another patrol out within a couple of hours of the first as a check system."

She turned in front of him, enough so he could see the outline of her lovely face. "I hope he has been buried. I don't wish to see his body or know what became of it. He's out of my life and I prefer it that way. I have no cause for goodbyes. I don't know how Steenie will react to the news when he knows all, but he's young. I'll help him deal with his loss. He did love his sire, even though he'd been disciplined more than he deserved. He struggled with that love, and now I fear this will be another challenge for him."

"Losing someone is difficult. I've seen many of our clan pass on in the last few years. We all have faults. It doesn't make losing someone any easier. I'd be happy to talk with him if you like. I lost someone dear to me not long ago, so I understand how difficult this will be for him."

"You did? I'm so sorry. Who was it? Would you like to talk about it?" She squeezed his hand.

Braden sighed, thinking about Ronan. "I had a good friend who took his own life."

"Oh, Braden, I'm so sorry."

"His family said it was because he believed his beloved had been unfaithful, but I don't understand. I don't think 'tis true. How I wish he'd talked to me before he did it. Sometimes I feel guilty because I didn't notice that he was sad or angry about something, but he must have been. How could I have been so blind?"

"I'm sure it had naught to do with you, but I understand. What he did made you feel powerless."

"In fact, I was so desperately guilty that I made a pact with God that I'd save two people's lives to make up for not being there when Ronan needed me most." He hadn't shared that with anyone before, and saying the words out loud made him feel lighter. It also made him feel even closer to Cairstine.

"You've upheld your end of the bargain, so 'tis time to let your guilt go."

"What?" He gave her a peculiar look because he couldn't follow her reasoning.

"You saved more than two. You saved me and Steenie and

a whole group of lassies. You've paid your debt. Release your guilt." She turned toward him and leaned in to kiss the underside of his chin, right where his small scar sat.

He hadn't looked at it quite like that, but while it wasn't solely on his shoulders, he *had* helped save the lassies. Did that absolve his guilt?

Nay, he hated to admit it, but it was still there.

"Tell me about your cousins. You never knew they survived?"

"Nay. The Lamonts kept me away from everything. I never spoke to anyone except the two of them. I knew the girls had been visiting Aunt Fina, but I never knew if the Lamonts killed everyone in the area. They were daft, all of them. 'Struth is my life revolved around Steenie for the last five years. I knew of naught but him."

"We need to make sure Maggie learns of their involvement in your aunt's murder. Edith said that some of them were different men. Who knows where they traveled from there."

"I pray Aunt Fina is still alive. Eva was traumatized from watching her mother die in front of her eyes. They are like me. They lost their parents and were then taken captive. That's a sad thing to have in common, isn't it? I never would have recognized Eva because she was so little the last time I saw her."

"You did right by Edith. 'Twas your voice calling her name that helped her focus. How did you recognize her if you have not seen her in six years?"

"Her sire taught all of us how to scream in a certain way to let our clan know if we were in trouble. In fact, 'tis one of my fondest memories with them. We lassies would scream as loud as we could, then giggle terribly. He would make us repeat it until we had just the right screech to our voices. Now I understand how invaluable that lesson was. I recognized her immediately. I'm so pleased to have found both of them."

When they finally arrived at Muir Castle, the gates were wide open, so Braden dismounted and helped her down. There was no one in the stables, though a few horses remained in their stalls. It had been several hours since their battle, and other than the random blood spatters, there was no other indication of the fight. He took her hand and headed toward the keep, his gaze scanning the area for any signs of life. There were none. Blood spatters could be seen, but the bodies had all been removed.

Cairstine's grip tightened on his hand, and her steps slowed as they moved across the courtyard. The silence was eerie, so he understood her hesitation. After all they'd been through, he expected someone to jump out at them at any moment. Muir Castle had a bloody history.

"Are you sure you wish to do this, sweeting? If you give me directions, I'll search your chamber, look for anything at all. Just tell me."

She shook her head, and he could tell she was doing her best to keep the tears at bay. He reached up and brushed a lone drop away with his thumb. "If you need to cry, go ahead. No reason to keep it all inside of you. No one will hear you but me."

"And the ghosts…" She stared up at the sky and closed her eyes, taking two deep breaths before she opened them again. "I need to go into my parents' bedchamber. Greer took that chamber, and I was never allowed in it. I was given one at the end of the passageway, one of our guest chambers. Greer had his men burn all my possessions except for a few wool gowns so there's naught there for me. But I'd like to see if anything of my parents' possessions remain."

"I'll check first if you'd like."

"Nay. I would prefer to go with you if you don't mind."

Holding her hand, he led her inside the darkened hall and up the stairs. She pointed out her parents' chamber and they moved down the passageway, but she stopped just outside the door. Lifting her gaze to his, she whispered, "I so wish to find something, anything, of theirs. Just a small token of their lives together, some keepsake that will always remind me of them. I searched all the years I was here, but never found anything. This is my last chance."

He leaned down to kiss her cheek and pushed the door open.

———◆———

CAIRSTINE FOUGHT TO HOLD THE bile in her throat back. Her parents' bedchamber was an absolute mess. Her mother would faint if she ever saw it in such a condition.

"Unbelievable that anyone could live in this. He was a swine, but I didn't realize that he literally preferred a sty. I'm so sorry, Cairstine." He moved ahead of her, kicking items away, moving them to the side.

"Are you looking for something in particular, Braden?"

"I just wish to make sure there are no critters in here. I'll leave the door open so they can run away, if so."

Cairstine couldn't stop the revulsion from showing on her face. The coverlet on the bed had been carefully stitched by her mother. Now it was covered with dirt and blood stains and unnamed bodily fluids. "The smell is so bad, I know not how long I can tolerate it. If we look through the chests and find naught, I'll be satisfied."

Braden pointed to one. "You go through that one, I'll go through this one on the floor. 'Tis more than likely to hold weapons. Be watchful for sharp items. I doubt he cared for his swords and daggers any better than he did his chamber."

Cairstine opened the doors on the chest, surprised to find a few neatly folded tunics inside along with some daggers. She was almost ready to give up when her hand reached into the far corner and discovered a box. Pulling it out, she gasped when she saw the top of it.

"Did you find something? I hope so, because there's naught in here but weapons. I'll put out the engraved ones in case they belonged to your sire or brother." Braden cleared an area on the bed and laid several items down.

She glanced quickly at the weapons but shook her head. "None belonged to my sire or my brother. But this box is familiar to me." She returned her attention to the box she'd found in the back of the chest. "My mother kept some of her jewelry in here. She did not have much, but she had a pearl necklace and a large emerald ring. She never wore them, only the ring given to her when they married." She held her breath and undid the clasp, lifting the wooden lid completely.

It was empty.

She wouldn't cry, she would *not* cry.

"I am so sorry, sweeting. You will keep the box? 'Twas something of your mother's." He wrapped his arms around her, and she rested her head against his chest, her hands still holding the cherished box.

"Aye, I have the box. 'Tis all I have, but 'tis something. I doubt there is aught else in this mess. They must have sold everything. Mama used to talk about a secret hiding place, but she never said where it was."

Braden stepped away from her, looking up at the ceiling. "Highlanders are well known for stashing valuables in case of a raid. My Grant ancestors built many hiding places inside our keep. Mayhap we need to look at it a wee bit differently. If your parents used a hidden place, Greer may never have seen it through this mess. Let's look at the floor."

They spent nearly an hour pushing the discarded clothing and weaponry aside so they could study the floor, but they found naught. She was sure she'd gotten her hopes up over nothing.

"Mayhap 'tis in the great hall or in the ceiling," he offered. He scratched his head and then stared up at the ceiling again. There was no sign of an opening or a loose area or anything that did not belong. "Or in the cellars."

When he dropped his gaze, he saw something unusual.

"What is it?" She followed his gaze and stared at the stone wall behind the bed, but nothing stood out to her.

"There," he pointed to a spot above the bed, nearly to the ceiling. "There's no packing around that stone. It could be just loose, but it could be…" He climbed up on top of the bed and moved carefully over to the wall. He wasn't as tall as many of his cousins, but he was still a tall man by Muir standards. The ceiling was so high that it was almost out of his reach, but he managed to wiggle the stone.

It scraped and moved easily, though it was bulky and looked heavy. He dropped it onto the bed and tried to peer inside the cavity it had protected.

Cairstine's stomach clenched when he turned around to smile at her. "There's something in there. I cannot tell what. Give me a few moments." He did his best to reach inside the spot, but she could tell he was struggling to achieve the right angle. What could be in there?

He hopped off the bed and said, "I'm going to put the chest in front. Help me move the bed back and I'll climb up."

Once they rearranged the furniture, Braden climbed atop of the chest and stuck his hand inside the opening. He hit soft wool first, so he tugged it out and held it up for Cairstine to see.

"My sire's dress plaid!" she squealed with delight.

He handed it to her and she smiled, running her hand across the finely woven silver threads and blue and green wool before bringing the garment up to rub it against her cheek.

"Mama insisted on sewing the silver threads herself. They were so proud of our heritage. I can see her hands in this, she worked tirelessly and diligently each time she made him a new one." She could remember seeing her sire in it whenever they had a special festival or a visit by the king. He had looked so regal and handsome, especially when he sat atop his warhorse. The memory brought a tear to her eye. Then she noticed something else. "Oh, Braden, it smells just like Papa did. He always reminded me of the outdoors—the horses, the pine trees. 'Tis almost like he's standing next to me again." She couldn't stop the tears, but these were tears of joy. For the first time in so long.

Braden reached up again, but this time he needed both of his hands to heft something out of the hole. The hilt of a sword. "Is this your sire's?"

"Aye. If there is engraving on the hilt."

"I believe there is, but 'tis well worn." He set it on the bed. "A fine weapon meant for a son. I think there is one more item." He reached in and pulled out a small box and handed it to her.

She didn't recognize the box, so she opened it and gasped. Her mother's wedding ring. Her hand shook when she pulled out the golden ring, a large rectangular blue sapphire set in the middle. She put it on her finger and smiled. "It fits perfectly."

"I'm sure your mother would want you to wear it. 'Tis quite beautiful. Let me check to see if there is aught else." He reached inside again, but this time came back with nothing. "I'm afraid we've reached the end of it." He lifted the stone that he'd dropped on top of the bed, and it made a strange sound. "Huh. This stone strikes me as unusual. I didn't notice that when I took it out." He climbed down from the bed and held out the stone for Cairstine's appraisal.

"I think these are hinges on the back, well-hidden." She scratched about with her finger and found a hidden latch.

"The stone is hollow. I wonder where they found it," she said as she peered inside.

"My guess is your sire had it built that way. What's inside?"

Cairstine pulled out a heavy red velvet pouch with

golden ribbon cinching it closed at the top. She loosened the ribbon and peeked inside, then lowered herself onto the bed and positioned her skirt just so. When she tipped the pouch upside down, a seemingly endless cascade of coins fell into her lap.

"Oh my, Braden. How much do you think this is worth? I know naught about coins." She picked up a few and let them trickle through her fingers.

He picked up two gold coins, taking a moment to examine them. "Good news. I'm quite sure you'll be able to restore this castle to exactly the way it was before the Lamonts arrived to do their damage."

Her eyes lit up and she nearly threw herself at him, but first she replaced the coins in the pouch and pulled the drawstring tight. The last thing she wished to do was to add to the mess Greer had left.

They gathered their items together and left the chamber, but Braden came to a sudden stop. "If you don't mind, I'm going to replace that stone in the wall. It seems like bad luck to leave it that way. I think your sire would want it put back to rights."

She was only alone for a moment, but a breeze came down the passageway, lightly blowing through her hair. She turned around and lifted her face to the ceiling because her sire's familiar aroma drifted past her again. Smiling, she closed her eyes. To her shock, it felt as if a hand cupped the back of her head, something her sire he had done so many times to her when she was young. A deep voice that wrapped her in a warmth that was only her sire's whispered, "He's the one, my wee flower."

She opened her eyes with a start and turned her head back toward her parents' bedchamber. Her sire had often called her that—his wee flower. The breeze stopped, and his presence drifted away. She whispered, "I know, Papa. Thank you for bringing him to me."

Her heart nearly burst when Braden came back into the

passageway. It felt as if her father had just validated what her heart already knew.

"Is everything all right?" he asked. "Were you talking to someone?"

"Nay, 'twas naught."

He kissed her head and took her hand, leading her down the staircase. While she trusted him completely, she would keep the moment she'd shared with her sire to herself. It hardly mattered whether it was real or not. To her, her sire had just spoken to her—and he'd let her know that her life was about to change for the better.

When they arrived in the great hall, they paused to sit at the trestle tables in the hall. She peered up at the bare walls and said, "I can have another tapestry hung there. My mother had made a beautiful one of Muir Castle in winter. Or mayhap I'll hang my sire's plaid there and have his sword hung above it as a remembrance.

Another breeze blew through her hair and she smiled, as if her sire had just nodded his approval.

Braden glanced over his shoulder. "Did you just feel a warm breeze?"

She nodded, unable to speak for fear she would tear up.

"The door is closed. Where would it come from?"

She reached for his cheek and gently turned his face back toward her. "It does not matter. What matters is you and I are here together. Will you return with me someday and help me hang my sire's sword on that wall?"

"Absolutely. 'Tis a fine place for it. I'm sure that would please your parents. Is there aught else you'd like to do while we're here?"

"Aye," she said, looking suddenly shy.

He quirked his brow at her, but he waited for her to explain.

"I'd love a bath. There's a tub in the kitchens. If you do not mind waiting, I'd like to wash all this grime from my skin and wash my hair. I want to start fresh. Do I sound daft?"

"You're sure you'd like to do it here? My aunt has a wonderful bathing chamber in the Grant keep. Will the memories be too much for you here?"

She squared her shoulders, thinking of her parents, her clanmates, all those who had perished here because of greed. "Nay. 'Tis time to take Muir Castle back. I am my sire's daughter, and this was my home, and I hope to make it thrive again someday. That starts now. I'll not cower to the Lamonts again."

"Your sire would be proud," he said, leaning over to take her lips with his. She parted her lips with a sigh, enjoying the closeness, the feeling of their tongues dueling. How she admired this man. He was everything she could ever want. He teased her with his tongue and she responded, but it wasn't enough. She wanted more from him. After all the horrid kisses Greer had given her, she wanted to erase the memory of him and fill her mind with new memories, memories of Braden Grant. She pulled back, panting, blushing at the strength of her ardor, though she was pleased to see his breathing matched hers.

"I'd truly love that bath first, if you don't mind." Her fingers rested on her lower lip as if she could save the kiss he'd given her.

"First?" Braden took her hand and squeezed it as he led her into the kitchens.

"Aye, first."

He grinned, kissed her cheek and piled wood in the hearth to start a fire. "This is a grand hearth your sire had made. I doubt 'twill take long to heat your water. Stay here and rest while I look belowstairs. Mayhap I'll find some whisky or ale, something to quench our thirst."

She said, "I'll see if I can find something to eat."

"Don't go far, temptress."

CHAPTER TWENTY

ONCE BRADEN GOT THE TUB settled for Cairstine, he left to give her the privacy and quiet she needed. He didn't want to go outside in case anyone returned to the keep, so he stayed within its doors. During his search of the cellars, he'd found a few things that he thought she might enjoy, so he decided to decorate her chamber. After several trips back and forth to her chamber at the end of the passageway, he was finally satisfied, and then ran out to the well to get himself enough water for a quick bath. He found a small tub, set it in front of the hearth in the hall, and suffered through the immersion in cold water.

As he set to scrubbing himself, he thought long and hard about his future with Cairstine, about what their lives might be like together. As he'd noticed before, thoughts of Cairstine brought a calm to his soul that he treasured. Now that calm was also bringing clarity.

He'd just gotten out of the bath when he heard her emerge from the kitchens. He grabbed his extra plaid and wrapped it around himself, but he left his tunic off. She wore a night rail, a beautiful white gown with roses sewn into the bodice and pink ribbons on the front, something delicate and feminine. Her beautiful, long hair was unbound, fanning out around her like a halo.

"You look beautiful. I must ask. Are you sure you wish to do this?" He stayed where he was, hoping she'd come to him. Knowing her history in this castle, he would never encourage her to do anything she wasn't completely ready to do.

She nodded. "I love you, Braden Grant. Whether you want it or not, I give you my heart and I trust you completely with it. I know this has been verra quick for you, so if you wish to wait, we will. I am also willing to take the risk that you may not fall in love with me. If that happens and you choose another, I will be grateful for our time together—and for all you have done for me."

Her words reached down to his soul and shook him. He reached for her and tucked her in his arms, resting his chin on the top of her head while he paused to think about what he wished to say. "I struggle for words as I'm not verra good with them, so I'll simply say this. I love you, Cairstine Muir. From the moment I saw you, I could hear what you were telling me with your eyes. That you needed to be saved. That you needed to be protected. And that you needed to be loved. And my body spoke in response to yours without my having to find the words. I vow to keep you safe, protected, and loved for the rest of my life."

She pulled back, a wide smile on her face. "Truly? I won't ask you to say it again. Once is enough for me. But you've made me verra happy, Braden Grant. We've been blessed to find each other."

He surprised her even more when he dropped to one knee. "Will you do me the honor of becoming my wife, Cairstine Muir?"

Tears misted her eyes, but she didn't hesitate. "Aye, I will."

He kissed her, searing her lips with his, deepening it to try to tell her how he truly felt. This was not something that would ever leave him. He knew they were meant to be together. A warm breeze blew across the hall, something they both noticed because they broke their kiss, looking toward the door for the source of the wind.

They found nothing.

Cairstine's gaze dropped to his chest and she gasped. "Oh, Braden."

He followed her glaze and glanced at his chest, just then realizing what she was seeing. His torso was covered with bruises and cuts from the beating he had taken from the Lamonts' men. She stepped close to him and ran her finger down a path between the worst of his bruises, passing through the dark hair on his chest until she reached his waist. Then she began to kiss each of his wounds. He threaded his fingers through her hair on her neck, being careful not to touch the swelling in her head, then closed his eyes to the sweetest torture he'd ever endured.

"Know that there is nowhere I would rather be than right here with you," he whispered. "When I first saw you on Drummond land, I thought you were the most beautiful woman I had ever seen." He ran his finger down her jawline and underneath her chin, tilting it slightly to lift her gaze to his. "And you must indeed be the strongest woman I've ever met. I know that I would like you by my side when we return. The idea of waking up with you in my arms every day makes me ecstatic. I don't wish to wait to marry." His lips dropped to hers and he gave her a soft kiss. "When you denied me? I've never felt such pain."

"Braden, I'm so…"

"Hush," he said. "You need not apologize. I know why you did it, and I'm proud of you for staying strong. I neglected to ask if you will allow me to be a sire to your son?"

"Aye," she whispered, giving him a soft kiss on his lips. The happiness in her green eyes, which had oft looked so sad, sent a wave of emotion through him. "Naught would make me happier. I'm sure Steenie will be thrilled to have you as his father."

"I wish I had a ring for you like the one your sire gave your mother. I will travel to Edinburgh someday soon and find a beautiful one for you. I promise."

She stood back with a stunned expression on her face. "Nay, you will not." She held her hand up, showing him her mother's sapphire ring. "This ring was from my sire's mother. 'Tis a Muir ring that has passed down through the generations. If not for you, Braden Grant, I would never have found it. We found this ring together, and it represents our love. Only a man who truly loves me would have had the patience to search my parents' chamber as you did. In my mind, my mother guided you to this ring. Can you accept that?"

He nodded. "Aye. 'Tis an heirloom that belongs on your finger, and we did find it together. Even I cannot explain why that stone caught my eye. Mayhap there are special forces guiding us. Many in my family would agree with you." So many people he knew believed in the spirits of angels or something similar—who was he to argue with them? And there was that gust of wind that had buffeted them twice in the empty castle...

He stepped closer and ran his hand down her arm, wishing to remove every separation between them. "I can accept that it represents our love. I will always remember it that way."

She held her ring up, turning it from side to side to show him how it sparkled, even inside. "I'd always admired this ring." She dropped her hand and whispered, "They must have left those things there before the clan was attacked. They guessed what would happen."

"Whatever they did, they did for you and your brother." He took her hand and kissed it, then said, "Come with me? I have something to show you." He led her upstairs to her chamber at the end of the passageway.

When they reached the room, she hurried toward him and threw her arms around his neck, kissing him deeply, teasing him the way he teased her. Leaving him no doubt that they would be good together.

He pulled back and said, "I like this part of you, but will

you come inside?"

She nodded, and he opened the door, allowing her to step inside first.

She gasped when she saw what he'd done.

He arranged a row of lit candles across the chest, and her bed was covered with Muir plaids.

"Where did you find them?" she asked as she moved over and settled her hand on the soft fabric. "They're so beautiful."

"They were stacked in a chest way in the back of the buttery, a place no one had ever looked, I would guess. I also found this." He reached for the bottle of wine he'd found in the cellars and poured two goblets for them, handing one to her before holding his own up to make a toast. "To our love and to our forever." He took a long swig from his goblet but then set it down, taking hers from her hand, too, and setting it down next to his.

"This waiting has tortured me, lass. I wish to touch you."

She reached for the ribbons on the front of her night rail but he stayed her hand.

"May I?"

She nodded, blushing.

He undid the fine ribbons, surprised to see his hands trembling, tugging on each one in a slow process that seemed akin to torture. "Mayhap I should have allowed you to do this. I'm not verra quick with it, am I?"

She settled her hands on his hips and took a step closer. "You are perfect for me, Braden Grant."

He arched his brow at her. "I hope you'll say that later."

She giggled and ran her hands up his abdomen, causing him to gasp in surprise, then she moved them up to his chest, running her fingers lightly across his skin.

"You'll not hurt me," he said, barely recognizing the huskiness of his voice.

"But the bruises…"

"You'll not hurt me, trust me." He grinned at her, then

glanced down at the protrusion showing in his plaid. "Do I look hurt?" His cock had hardened the moment he'd touched the first ribbon. "There. I think I've undone the last of them. May I touch your skin now?"

She nodded, and said one word, "Please."

How he wished to do this right. He knew she wasn't a virgin—indeed, her experience probably outstripped his own—but her experiences with Greer Lamont had likely not been pleasant. He wanted more than anything to show her how it was supposed to be.

He could ask her about her experiences, about what she liked or disliked, but he didn't want either of them to think about the awful man who'd so ignored her will and wishes. This night was to be about them.

He cradled her face in his hands and captured her lips with his, a slow, sensual kiss that he intended as proof of how much he desired her. She tilted her head back, telling him her desire equaled his own. His tongue circled hers in a carnal dance, tasting her sweet cavern. His hands moved to her hair, slowly massaging her scalp as they moved down through the damp strands, separating them until they cascaded down her back and over her shoulders.

"I'm not hurting you, am I?" he whispered, aware of the swelling still there.

"Nay, your touch is wonderful."

He moved his mouth across her jawline to her neck, trailing a line of kisses down across her shoulders as he moved her night rail down, his hands sliding it off her shoulders and, with the lightest of touches, down her sides until it dropped and pooled at her feet. His hands moved to her breasts, cupping both of the pert mounds until his tongue followed, eager to taste each pink crown.

Cairstine whimpered the softest of sounds as he continued to pleasure her breasts, paying close attention to each areola, each nipple until she grasped his shoulders, her nails digging into his flesh.

To his surprise, she tugged on the broach of his plaid, dropping it to the floor, and fell to her knees in front of him, gripping him in her hand before she followed with her tongue. She lapped the head of his cock before making long strokes down the length of him. He fought not to finish in her mouth, fought not to wrap his hands into her hair because he feared she'd misinterpret his movements as force.

Everything she did with him would be of her own free will. Always.

He groaned when she took him full in her mouth. When he could take it no more, he lifted her to her feet and then scooped her into his arms and set her on the bed. She squealed and smiled, even more so when he said, "You're torturing me, and I'll not lose it like a laddie our first time."

He kissed her again and moved his hands to the vee between her legs, pleased to find her slick with juices for him. He teased her folds until she spread wide for him, then slipped his fingers inside, moving in a rhythm to tease her, make her want more.

"Braden, please. I want more of you…'tis so different." She tilted her hips toward him in a small, trusting movement that absolutely humbled him.

He gripped her hips and moved over her, settling his cock at the sweet juncture of her thighs. He breached her in one swift movement, and she moaned as he filled her completely. As he began to stroke in and out of her, stretching her to take all of him, she grasped his hips in a frenzy, pushing him into a pace that nearly forced him over the edge, but he would not finish before her. Her molten heat spread all around him, welcoming him inside her.

Hell, but they were wonderful together.

———•———

CAIRSTINE THOUGHT SHE WOULD EXPLODE. Braden made her feel things she'd never experienced before. She wanted to share this with him because her mother had told her this was what married couples do, but she'd had no idea it would be a totally pleasurable experience because it never had been before. This was the man she loved, and every touch, every stroke, brought her pleasure she hadn't imagined possible. Indeed, he couldn't move fast enough to suit her. She grabbed his hips, moving her pelvis in the rhythm she wanted; no, that she needed. She trembled with a fever she didn't understand but couldn't stop.

"More, Braden. I know not what I want for certain, but more…please…"

He plunged into her, thrusting and thrusting over and over again until she thought she would die from the need pulsating inside her. He drove into her with an urgency that she shared, and they moved together in a beautiful beat that brought her to tears.

When she thought she would lose her mind, he reached down and touched her in just the right spot, caressing her until she screamed as her insides shattered, catapulting her over the edge. Her body thrummed with exquisite pulses of pleasure as he continued his strokes, extending her peaks. Then he gave a ferocious roar as he experienced his own climax.

All she could do was stare at him in awe as she fought to control her own breathing. He held himself up on his elbows, kissing her neck, her cheek, her lips, and sucking on her lower lip just a bit before he collapsed on the side of her.

He stroked the curve of her cheek with his thumb, a soft caress that he continued as he stared at her.

She could stare at him for hours.

The man held her and touched her so reverently it was as if he worshipped her. Her breasts still pressed against him, she could feel the hammering of his heart inside, the power of that beat strictly for her. She wished to shout to the world how happy she was lying here in Braden Grant's arms.

Before this day, she'd thought of this act as something horrible, something to dread, to hate. With Braden, the act was beautiful and special, an act of giving and receiving, so magnificent, she'd had no idea the possibility existed.

"I love you," she whispered, strictly because she could think of nothing else that fit the moment. The way he treated her was such a declaration of his love that it just felt right to say it again.

"I love you, too. I pleased you, lassie?"

She couldn't help but giggle. "Lassie? I'm hardly a lassie, but aye, you pleased me in so many ways." She thought for a moment, wondering how to tell him this was the first time she'd experienced pleasure. "Umm…'twas verra different with you."

"Have you never climaxed before?"

"Nay," she blushed.

He brushed his thumb across her bottom lip. "Do not be embarrassed. 'Tis probably wrong, but that fact pleases me. In fact, I could crow about it, but I'd not do that to you, just know that you made my chest puff out a wee bit."

She giggled, but the giggle turned into laughter, something she hadn't done in a long time. "Will you feel the same way every time I climax?" The need to touch him hadn't diminished, so she ran her hands through the short dark hairs smattered across his chest, surprisingly alluring to her.

He smirked, rolled his eyes, and said, "Aye, probably. 'Tis naught wrong with loving to see your pleasure, is there?"

"Nay." She decided to change the subject and snuggled against him. "What do you think will happen to Muir Castle now?"

He tipped her chin up so he could gaze into her eyes directly. "You are the only heir to this castle. My uncle and sires will see that it stays in your clan."

"But if I'm the only one…Would you consider living here with me after we're married?"

He moved his hand behind his head, staring up at the ceiling. "Uncle Alex had mentioned he might be interested in taking it over if 'twere empty. This was before we came to investigate and found the Lamonts here. He said the fields are not that fertile because of the foundation and the way it was built, but I think he would allow us to live here. He gave my brother Loki his own castle and he's laird, though 'tis small with verra few clanmates. They're still part of Clan Grant, so Uncle Alex assists them with anything they need. I'm sure he'll confer with our king, but there are no sons of your father. I think once we marry the king would grant us this castle."

Her eyes lit up. "And you can be chieftain of all that is here?"

He chuckled. "Me? Chief?"

"Aye, why not? Your uncle was a laird, and your cousins are."

"I'd be laird of five of us." He grinned. "You, me, Steenie, mayhap Corc and Hilda if they return with us. I like that idea. I might be able to handle five people."

She moved up onto her elbows and rolled onto her belly to stare at him. "Aye. If anyone wished to join us, we would welcome them. Mayhap Aunt Fina is hale, and she could move here with Eva and Edith. Anyone else who wished to join us would just have to pitch in like we all did when it was Clan Muir. We could get Corc to handle the stables, and Hilda to tend to the kitchens, and a few others to work the fields. I know there are not many, but we had oats and turnips and carrots, even a small apple orchard that has been ignored. Could you imagine if we had our own bairns and raised them here with our own clan…" She paused and her face curled into a frown.

"You mean Clan Muir?" he asked.

"Or Clan Grant?" she added.

Braden chewed on the inside of his mouth for a moment. "I would guess Uncle Alex would say Clan Grant. That would guarantee the help of his guards if we ever needed them. He gave Loki a small group to start with. They even built a few cottages, helped to rebuild Castle Curanta."

"I could live with that, but with one caveat."

"Before you say aught, think about this. Are you willing to be known as a Grant instead of a Muir?"

Still on her belly, she kicked her feet up and down on the bed while she gave it some thought. This was a most difficult question.

She had heard of the Drummonds. Diana was laird of the Drummonds, but her husband Micheil had kept his Ramsay name. In fact, Drummond land was where she'd first set eyes on Braden, though they hadn't formally met until outside the castle. Would Braden ever consider such a thing? But she decided quickly it was not what she wished for them. Her mother had become a Muir, so it was only right that she would become a Grant. Besides, she rather liked the idea of a fresh start.

"I'm willing to be a Grant, and I know Steenie would be. I would ask for one thing, for this to be forever known as Muir Castle, since 'twas my clan who built it."

"I can't argue with that. 'Tis most reasonable. I'll speak to my uncle after we arrive back on Grant land."

CHAPTER TWENTY-ONE

B RADEN HADN'T FELT THIS CONTENTED in a long time. It was near dusk when they arrived on Grant land. The moon was nearly full with few clouds, so they could look at the stars as they came into view. They spent quite a bit of time trying to identify the familiar shapes in the sky.

When they were almost back, Braden noticed an approaching horse out of the corner of his eye. It was headed toward the cliffs.

"Did you see them?" he asked her.

"Aye, but I did not get a good look at them. A lad and a lass, I think. Did you know them?"

"I think one was Marta, Ronan's betrothed." What the hell would Marta be doing leaving the castle at this hour? He decided to investigate. He started to follow them but then changed his mind, heading toward the gates instead. "I think I know where they are headed. Would you mind finding my cousin Roddy or my brother Loki and sending them after me? I may need assistance with this, though I have no idea who I'll find or where they are going."

She nodded, then slid off the horse as they reached the gates. "I'll find them right away. Please be careful, Braden."

"I will. Tell them I headed toward the cliffs."

She nodded and he took off in the direction the couple had been headed. Hellfire, but he could swear he'd seen

Marta on that horse, though he had not recognized the man behind her.

Had it been her secret lover? He needed to find out. Mayhap it would finally give him answers to the question that continued to niggle at him about Ronan's death.

He drove his horse hard, hoping to catch them. He was nearly to the cliffs when he heard a woman scream. It had to be the lass on the horse. No one else would be out here at such a late hour. He pushed forward, surprised at the situation he came upon. The two had dismounted and the man was dragging the woman toward the cliffs against her will. She squirmed and fought him, but he was obviously much stronger than her.

"Stop where you are!" Braden bellowed, hoping to slow the man's progress. Who the hell was it?

"Come any closer and I'll throw her over at once." He finally turned around, but he was too far away for Braden to recognize him. He looked in three different directions until his gaze finally settled on Braden. Deliberately disobeying him, the man took several steps closer to the cliffs.

Braden hurried toward them, intent on stopping him, unsheathing his sword. Losing Ronan had been devastating. He would not let his friend's beloved meet the same horrible fate. After ten steps, Braden finally recognized the man, and he was so shocked and furious that he ran straight toward the two of them.

"Keith, you bastard. Let her go at once!"

"Please, Braden," Marta cried. "Stop him. I don't want to die. He's going to kill me!" Marta was sobbing and could barely stand up.

He halted once he realized how tenuous the situation was. "Let her go, Keith. Why would you want to hurt her? She would have married Ronan. She would have been your sister." Braden had no notion of what Keith wanted, but he knew he needed to distract him and keep him talking. He moved a few steps closer.

"No more, Grant. I swear I'll toss her over. Drop your weapon." The look on his face was unwavering. Braden didn't hesitate to let his sword fall to the ground. It would take careful persuasion to get Keith to change his mind. He was staunchly resolved in his plan.

Suddenly, it dawned on him. Keith had done this before. "You killed him, didn't you? Ronan didn't take his own life at all."

Horse hooves echoed behind him, and he turned his head enough to see Roddy and Loki come to a stop behind him. He held his hand out to them, indicating they should stop.

He had to get the answer to his question. "All along, 'twas you, was it not? You tried to convince me and everyone else that I was the guilty party, that 'twas my fault Ronan threw himself to his death, but he didn't, did he?"

Marta sobbed and shook her head. "He killed my Ronan. Ronan…" Her pained wails seemed to echo in the night air.

"Why? Why would you kill your own brother, Keith? *Why?*"

Braden kept an eye on his weapon, hoping to see an opening. As he'd moved closer to Keith, the bastard had moved closer to the edge of the cliffs. He now held a dagger at Marta's throat with a tight grip on her arm.

"One more step, Grant, and I'll toss her over. She's much lighter than my brother."

"Why?" He still could not understand. Then it dawned on him what had probably caused him to act this way, so he changed tactics. He glanced at Marta pointedly, hoping she would catch on to what he was doing. Hoping she would trust him. "I can see in her eyes that Marta loves you. We all could see it. Why would you hurt the woman who loves you?"

"She doesn't love me. I told Ronan I loved her, but he wanted her for himself. He wouldn't stay away. I warned him…I warned him many times, but he always takes everything I desire. He told me they were in love."

He gave Marta a scathing look and then said, "And she figured it out. Came at me screaming today when I confessed my love for her. Is that any way to treat the man who loves you?"

Braden placed his hands behind his back, motioning for Loki to take out his slinger. They'd played with it so often when they were younger they'd formed the silent signal to avoid their parents' detection. Loki would no doubt interpret the movement correctly. He just needed to keep Keith talking and get him to step away from the cliff.

"Marta does love you. Isn't that right, Marta? I can see it in her eyes, in the way she looks at you." He stared at her again, hoping she would play along.

"I do," she gasped, though not convincingly. "I love only you, Keith. I'm sorry to have fussed about Ronan. You… you did what you had to do."

"Ronan, that daft fool. I told him many times. I warned him. She's mine." Then his voice softened as if he'd just absorbed her words. "You do, Marta? I told him you loved me. That you would be with me if only he'd step out of the way. I followed him out here when he was hunting. I just wanted to convince him to stay away, but he wouldn't listen to me." He kissed her cheek, hugging her close.

Braden shuffled to the side, hoping to give Loki better aim.

Marta cried, staring at Braden. "I love you, Keith. Please don't push me over."

"If you'd said that long ago, I would never have hurt him. I could have been the one to make you happy, take care of you."

His unpredictable rage unfurled again, this time focused on Braden. "I tried to convince everyone it was your fault, but nay. You're Braden Grant. You'd never try to steal Marta for yourself. You'd never upset Ronan to the point that he'd hurt himself. Then she—" he yanked Marta closer to stick the dagger back near her throat, "—she told Moray she thought one of us did it. I have to shut her up. I've no choice."

His anger was a terrible thing, and Braden couldn't help but reflect that he'd allowed his own anger to control him before. It was an uncontrollable beast, untethered rage.

Braden said, "No reason at all, Keith. I know a perfect cottage where you and Marta can live together. No one will ever bother you there." He motioned behind his back for Loki to take his shot. They were running out of time. "You can live there together forever. Don't you want to have her all to yourself? Have beautiful bairns with her? Which would you like first, a lad or a lassie?"

Keith smiled, and his grip lightened on Marta's neck. "What would you like first, love? A wee lass or a…"

Loki's slinger swished behind him and a second later, Keith grabbed his bollocks with a roar. Braden leaped on him, pulling Marta toward him and then pushing her back toward Roddy. Before Braden could get to his dagger, Keith tried to stab him, but he cut Braden's hand instead. The sight of blood pouring out of Braden's hand set Keith off in a tirade and he dropped his weapon.

"Look what you've done, Grant! This is all your fault. Why didn't you stay the hell away from us? She would've loved me eventually. I could have convinced her." He went straight at Braden's waist, trying to knock him down, but Braden was stronger.

The two wrestled until they were both on the ground near the edge of the cliff, throwing fists and punches in the tussle. Braden managed to pummel Keith's belly while the bastard retaliated by catching Braden square in his jaw.

Marta screamed, "Nay, Keith! Do not hurt Braden."

Braden had him in a choke hold because he could see Loki and Roddy moving closer, trying to find an angle where they could use their sword on Keith, but the daft man was fueled by a wild rage. Once he freed himself from Braden's grip, he stood and reached down to retrieve the dagger still on the ground when Loki managed to swing his sword close enough to catch the bastard across the belly. Keith dropped the dagger, staring at them in shock before he dropped his gaze to his belly, blood pouring out of the wound and staining his tunic. His knees buckled and he nearly fell forward, but at the last second, he teetered backward over the edge of the cliff, falling to his death.

Almost as if he'd done it intentionally.

Braden glanced at his palm, checking to see how serious the wound was across his hand.

Marta squealed and ran into Roddy's arms while Loki helped Braden up. He ripped a strip from his plaid and wrapped it tight across Braden's hand.

"Well done, negotiator," Loki smiled. "You gave me the perfect opening."

"Well done? He threw himself over to his own death," Braden said, putting pressure on the linen across his wound.

"I struck him deep enough for that to be a mortal wound. He'd not have survived."

"Mayhap so, but I'd hoped to save him. I was thinking of his surviving brother and his mother. They just lost another," Braden said, rubbing the back of his neck with his good hand.

"Cut you pretty good first, did he not? What would have been a better ending? If you'd grabbed him and taken him back, the lairds would have had to hang him in front of everyone. He killed a clanmate, his own brother, for no good reason. *And* tried to kill Marta. He would have killed you without a second thought."

Braden took a moment to mull over Loki's words.

"He's right," Roddy said. "His mother has already dealt with one loss. She can handle this one better than if she'd had to watch him hang in front of her. This was much kinder—for his mother, for Moray, and even for Keith himself. He knew 'twas the only way. I saw it that he threw himself over after he'd been stabbed, knowing the alternative."

"Marta, did he hurt you at all?" Loki asked.

"Nay, he just frightened me. I still cannot believe it." Her face was pale with shock.

"Me neither," Braden said, as he headed back to his horse, but he stopped, frozen for a moment.

The realization finally hit him that Ronan had not taken his own life.

He had not misread Ronan's signs. There had been none. His friend had been murdered. Just like that, an enormous weight of guilt was lifted off his shoulders.

CHAPTER TWENTY-TWO

WHEN THEY MADE IT BACK to Grant land, there was a small group awaiting them outside the stables. Steenie ran toward them, throwing his arms around Braden's legs and shouting, "You made it."

Cairstine was directly behind Steenie. She leaned over to kiss him while Steenie hugged him. "You hurt your hand? I was so worried!"

"Och, 'tis naught. I'll have Aunt Caralyn sew it up. She's our healer."

Marta's parents, nearly overcome with relief, embraced her and led her off to their cottage. Only after they left did Braden notice Moray and his mother standing off to the side of the gathering, worry etching both of their faces.

Braden gave Cairstine a kiss and said, "I'll explain everything inside, but I need to speak to someone first." He nodded toward Ronan's mother and brother.

Without pressing for more information, she squeezed him again and then took Steenie's hand and headed inside. Once again, her trust humbled him.

He trudged over to Ronan's surviving family, filled with sadness that he had yet more bad news to share with them. Moray said, "Keith was daft, was he not?" He had his arm on his mother's shoulder. The woman peered up at Braden with such hope, he didn't know how to break the news to her. Loki came along behind him, thank goodness, and set his hands on his shoulders and said, "Braden saved Marta's life. Roddy and I were there when Keith threatened to throw her over the cliff. He admitted to killing Ronan because he was in love with Marta. I'm so sorry."

The poor woman fell against her only remaining son, sobbing into his arms. Braden said the only thing he could think to say. "I'm so sorry."

"Don't be," Moray objected. "'Twas not your fault. I'm sorry Keith tried to make you suffer for something he did…and I'm even sorrier I believed him for a time. I'd seen the change in him, but I ignored it. Mama, I feel a wee bit better knowing Ronan didn't take his own life, though it's difficult to believe that Keith would have taken the life of his own brother. Now we have answers."

"I'm sorry, Braden. You were a good friend to Ronan and to all my boys. I know this is just as hard on you as it is on us," she sniffled. All he could think to do was hug her. When he pulled away, Moray clapped him on the shoulder and ushered her back toward their cottage.

"Thanks, Loki," Braden said, turning to his brother. "I wasn't quite ready for that yet. We'll do what we can for them, will we not?"

"Aye, always."

Their mother and father, Celestina and Brodie Grant, joined them after Ronan's family left. "Oh, Braden, we just heard what happened. I'm so sorry. Goodness, you have quite a wound there. I'll tell Aunt Caralyn you need stitching," their mama said. "We can talk later."

"Aye, thanks, Mama. This cut continues to ooze," he said, studying his skin under the blood-soaked fabric.

Celestina leaned in close and said, "Braden Grant, before I go, we just met a lovely woman with a beautiful ring on her finger. Are you betrothed? Your father thinks you could be. Did you forget to tell us?"

"I am." He grinned as his father clasped his shoulder. "In fact, I never understood how Papa knew you were the one when he first met you, Mama, but I've seen the truth of it now."

"Och, many do not believe in love at first sight, but we know better." His sire gave his mother's shoulder a squeeze and kissed her cheek. "Don't ignore what your heart tells you, even if it doesn't make sense to you."

"Cairstine has an unusual effect on me. For some odd reason, she calms me," he said, thinking about the truth of that statement, about how it had just seemed right the first time she was in his arms.

"You cannot deny the implication of that, son. You must be verra good together."

His mother said, "She is wonderful. The poor lass has had a traumatic few years, but she's obviously a strong woman and an even better mother. Loki filled us in while you were gone. I think you'll suit perfectly, and I adore Steenie, though Cairstine tells me he doesn't yet understand that his sire is gone for good."

"We'll help him through it," he said as they made their way back into the great hall. Braden stepped inside, pleased at the sight in front of him. The wee lassies they'd helped save sat near the hearth, hugging various fabric dolls and animals. The fear had left their eyes, and though he knew they would not recover so quickly, at least they were being given the chance to be bairns again.

Maggie and Cairstine joined him, and Will headed in their direction. "We did it again. Another group of wee lassies saved," Maggie said, glancing over her shoulder at the group of bairns.

"Have you learned aught more about the group?"

Maggie shrugged. "I haven't asked much yet. The lassies have been held for a few days. They were kept in cramped conditions at Muir Castle, without much food. We decided 'twas best to let them be bairns for a while. Your sisters and your cousins have all arranged to sleep in one big chamber with them to help them along. We'll get to the questions another day. My thanks for your assistance in this. I'm hoping Hilda and Corc can help, but I think she was overwhelmed. On the morrow is soon enough."

"I owe all of you my gratitude," Cairstine said. "You have saved us all."

Braden took her hand. "I don't know if you've heard, but I've asked Cairstine to be my wife."

Maggie and Will smiled and congratulated both of them. "We wish you all the best," Maggie said, giving them each a hug. "I thought there was something between the two of you, but I hadn't expected it to progress so quickly." She gave Will a saucy look, "But then, we know all about quick weddings, do we not?"

Will tugged her back against him, kissing her cheek from behind. "Aye, we do. But I've never regretted it for a moment. Why wait was my belief. I'd lived alone for a long time."

Maggie reached for Cairstine's hand and lowered her voice so she wouldn't be overheard. "After all you've been through, you deserve a wonderful man. You've found one. I'm happy for both of you." They stood back and stepped away to give them some privacy.

Braden hugged Cairstine to him and they turned around to greet the rest of the clan in the hall, but strangely enough, they were all involved in small groupings of lively conversations.

"You need not tell me all, but what exactly happened at the cliffs?"

He sighed, thinking of all that had transpired in a day. "Ronan and his brother were in love with the same woman. It made Keith daft. He killed Ronan and was about to kill Marta when I came upon them."

"Oh, Braden," she gasped. "How awful. But you and Loki and Roddy stopped him?"

"Aye. 'Twas such a shock to me, though I was right that Ronan did not take his own life."

"You were a good friend to him. You would have known if he were depressed."

He took a deep breath and wrapped his arm around her shoulder. "Aye, 'tis true." He touched his forehead to hers. "Why do I like having you here so much?"

She stood back and whispered, "I surely hope it stays that way." Her gaze scanned the hall. "You have a large clan, Braden."

"I do," he said, kissing the top of their head. "Do you think you'll mind becoming a part of this group?"

Steenie and Kenzie were giggling as the older lad imitated shooting their enemies with a slinger. Moments later, Steenie was running around with his arms extended, pretending to be a falcon.

"I can think of naught I'd rather do than to marry you and become a part of your family. Look how happy Steenie is. It's been a long time since I've seen him laugh like that. 'Tis hard to believe how much our lives have changed for the better since I saw you at the Drummond celebration."

"I think he'll be happy here. If you had a wish, what would it be?" Braden asked her, running his finger down her jawline and her neck.

"I know exactly what it would be. I'd wish that we could live the rest of our days at Muir Castle as part of Clan Grant, and that someday we'll be exactly like that couple over there." She tipped her head toward the couple whispering and kissing in the corner of the hall.

Braden smiled at the sight of them. "That's our laird. Uncle Alex and Aunt Maddie. He shares the lairdship with their eldest twins, who aren't here at the moment. I wish the exact same, because if it were to come true, we'd be happy and in love forever."

Aunt Maddie giggled and Uncle Alex picked her up and plopped her on his lap.

Cairstine whispered, "I couldn't ask for more than that. Well, there is one more thing I might ask…"

"If I can, 'tis yours."

"Release your guilt over Ronan. I could see how it bogged you down at Muir Castle. You saved Marta, which adds one more person to your list, but more importantly, Ronan didn't take his own life. There is no blame you could possibly place on yourself. Can you let it go?"

He squeezed her shoulders as he considered her words, and then nodded with a quick, "Aye."

He decided he could indeed let his guilt go. Ronan had been a great friend, and he would always miss him. With a surprised sense of clarity, Braden recognized that someone important had come into his life, and he wished to devote all his energy to this new relationship, because he wanted her happiness more than anything.

He kissed her forehead and whispered, "I love you, and I'm quite certain I know exactly how to define love. 'Tis my feelings for you."

EPILOGUE

———◆———

Two months later…

BRADEN AND CAIRSTINE WERE IN the Muir great hall. Eva and Edith were also along, and they were going to live in a hut with Aunt Fina once the place was made livable again. The three of them were in the bailey looking over the cottages, choosing their own to live in. Aunt Fina had been so overwrought when she'd come home to find them gone, but she'd been ecstatic to see the lassies again, and Cairstine had her dear aunt back. How pleased Cairstine was that she'd found someone else from her clan to inhabit their castle with them again.

Braden's parents were upstairs with Steenie cleaning out her parents' bedchamber. Cairstine had told his mother she couldn't bear to go into the room until it was cleared out. It reminded her too much of Greer.

His parents had said it was a wedding gift from them and they'd brought a couple of servants along to assist with the cleanup. They would take care of the chamber upstairs and make it as beautiful as it had once been. Cairstine had agreed, but he could tell she'd struggled to contain her tears.

"I love your parents, Braden. They remind me of my own. How I miss them." She was on her knees by the hearth, cleaning the floor around it. She and Braden had already cleaned what they could of the interior. She was quite certain it hadn't been cleaned since her parents had passed. When she finished with the floor, she moved to the mantle above the hearth, finding a fresh cloth to wipe the dirt and dust from the shelf above the stone and the soot that seemed to be everywhere.

They'd married quietly, with just the immediate Grant family and her cousins and Aunt Fina in attendance because Cairstine had been embarrassed about having a child of five winters without being married. As Braden had promised her, no one had cared.

His parents came down the stairs carrying a great big coverlet. "Cairstine, did your mother do this work?" Celestina asked. "'Tis quite beautiful."

"I know," she said, her face falling. "How it saddens me to have to throw it away."

"Throw it away? Why would you want to do that?"

"Gr…" she stopped herself, glancing over her shoulder at Braden, who quirked his brow at her. She'd asked him to never mention the *bastart*'s name again, and he'd agreed. "I feared 'twas ruined."

"I wished to ask you about it. Each of these patches appears to be a different plant. Was your mother into gardening?"

"Aye," she replied, doing her best to keep the tears from misting in her eyes. "She planted many herbs, and she had a beautiful garden near the side wall at one time. It smelled so sweet that I used to love to go there with her. I have many fond memories of her garden, though there's naught left of it now."

"Her needlework is exquisite," she murmured as she studied the fine stitches. "If you'd like, I'd be happy to take a look at the garden, see if we could restore it."

"Do you think 'tis possible?" She couldn't help but be hopeful about such an undertaking. Bringing her mother's garden back to life would be wonderful. She wished to have her mother's beautiful touches back in the castle, both inside and out.

"We can take a look at it on the morrow. Many plants reseed themselves."

Braden said, "Mama makes fragrant oils from lavender and other plants. She's quite skilled at it."

"That sounds lovely. I'd love to learn how you do that, and I've often wished for a garden of my own."

"Then 'tis settled. Steenie can help us dig in the dirt when we get started on it. But for now, we'll finish restoring the inside, and I think this coverlet will be stunning again." Celestina stopped and held it up. "I think it needs a good beating outside to get rid of the surface dirt, but I think we can wash it and get rid of nearly all the stains. I just need a large tub and my husband's help so I don't fall inside." She giggled like a young lass when she glanced up at Braden's sire. "If there are any stains left, your mother sewed it in pieces, so you could easily replace just one piece of fabric if need be. Maddie has plenty of extra fabric. In fact, she'd love to help you restore it once we wash it."

"I would love that," she said, her eyes lighting up.

"I hope we don't impose," Braden's sire said, "but the tower is in beautiful shape. It looks as if it hasn't been used in quite a while."

"It has not been used in several years," Cairstine said. Once again, Braden could hear the note of sadness in her voice, and he reached out and took her hand.

"If you don't agree, please say so," his sire said, "but Celestina and I have been talking, and the Grants have outgrown the keep, even with all the additions we've made. Would you consider allowing us to move here? We could live in the tower room as we do at Clan Grant. Our moving would free up space for some of the younger couples. This tower also has three levels so your sisters could have their own rooms, Braden."

Braden's mother glanced at Cairstine and said, "You know how we adore Steenie. We'd miss him terribly."

As if on cue, Steenie came barreling down the staircase shouting, "Grandmama, Grandpapa, you should see all the dirt I swept up! I filled the bucket all by myself." He rushed over to his mother and hugged her. "Everything looks better, Mama. We're fixing it just for you."

Cairstine glanced at Braden, nodding her head just a touch. Braden assumed it meant that she heartily approved of the plan. He knew how much she'd enjoyed being a part of a family again these last months, and he had to admit he'd prefer to have the castle fuller.

"I think it sounds wonderful," he said. "We'd love to have you stay with us. 'Tis a good-sized hall and keep. Not the same as Uncle Alex's, but we'll be lonely if we don't have family close."

"Steenie, what do you think?" Cairstine asked with a big smile on her face. "Would you like Grandmama and Grandpapa to stay here with us?"

Steenie jumped with joy and hugged his grandparents. "Aye. Can I sleep in the tower sometimes and then in my own chamber sometimes?"

"Aye, your aunts will come along, too."

The door opened and Loki came in with his family—his wife Bella, his sons Kenzie and Lucas, and their newly adopted daughter Ami. "Did I hear you correctly, Papa? You're moving here?"

"Aye, we'll be closer to your land from here, too."

Bella hugged Cairstine and set Ami down. "We came to help restore the keep."

"Nay, Bella!" Loki bellowed. "Kenzie, Lucas, and I came to help. You're to sit in that chair right by the hearth. Your only job is to keep an eye on Ami, though she has plenty of room to run in here."

"As you wish, Loki. We brought some bread, cheese, and mead, enough for the group." Bella grinned, rubbing her slightly rounded belly. "I cannot wait to see if this will be a lassie or a laddie."

The chatter continued as they helped Bella settle her gifts on the table, so Loki said, "Roddy is outside, Braden. He wished to speak to both of us, if you don't mind."

Braden kissed Cairstine's cheek and headed to the door. "I'll be right back."

"You like that Mama and Papa will be here?" Loki asked, once they were far enough away not to be overheard.

Braden hunched his shoulders up against the winds. Autumn was on its way and a chill had already entered the air. "I do. 'Twill make the place more of a home, and if I have to leave on patrol or go off with the Band of Cousins, I don't want Cairstine to be alone."

Loki grinned at him. "She's tough enough."

"She is, but I hope someday we'll have a bairn of our own. I'll be glad to have Mama around to help if that day comes."

"Good point."

"What does Roddy want?"

Loki just shrugged his shoulders in response.

They approached the stables where Roddy waited for them. Once he saw them, he stepped inside, taking cover from the cold Highland wind.

"Something wrong, Roddy?" Braden asked. "You're standing out here like a lost soul who can't decide what to do next."

Roddy scrubbed the stubble of his beard before he spoke. "I've got news, Braden. Maggie and Will were just at Grant Castle."

"You should have contacted me," Braden said. "We could have come over to visit."

Roddy shook his head. "They were in too much of a hurry. They needed to get a message to us."

"What is it?"

"They've learned of two more branches of the Channel

of Dubh. One of them runs to Edinburgh and the other connects to the loch where we found Steenie. She and Will are going to handle the Edinburgh one. She wondered if we would learn aught we could about this one. There are three or possibly four of us. What do you think?"

"Did you speak with Connor?"

"Aye, he'll go along with whatever we decide."

Loki said, "I can assist if it's close to this area, but Bella's expecting again. With Lucas and wee Ami still so young, I don't wish to leave her for long, especially after what happened last Christmas. After we lost the last one, I think my place is home until she gives birth."

Braden said, "Understood. I'll speak with Cairstine, but I know what she'll say. After nearly losing Steenie and the girls to those bastards, she'll send me with her blessings. Will we have enough men? I hope to have some guards soon. I've already talked with my parents and Cairstine. We just have to speak with Uncle Alex. We thought of inviting one family to join us."

"Who?" Loki asked.

"I thought to invite Ronan's family. Mayhap Moray would consider being my second in charge and could bring his mother here, settle in one of our cottages."

Roddy said, "I think 'tis a great idea. Moray appears lost, and in a sense, he is. Losing two brothers within a few months is difficult. I think he would enjoy settling somewhere new."

Loki said, "And she must be struggling with all the memories. She used to be a cook in the kitchens, and a great one, if my memory serves me well."

Braden snorted. "You would know with your appetite. You ate everything you could the first few months you joined us. Uncle Alex used to watch to see if you'd ever stop."

Loki gave him a sideways glance. "Still haven't stopped. Never mind that. You have plenty of room, true?"

"Aye. We have five plus the stables and a building for an armorer or blacksmith. Corc and Hilda are in the smallest one near the stables. Cairstine's aunt will take one to live in with Edith and Eva, so we still have three more."

"Corc and Hilda? Are they happy here now that they've married?" Roddy asked.

"Aye. They love it now that the Lamonts are gone, and they dote on Steenie. They were delighted to have their own place. Steenie is finally getting the attention he deserves between my parents and Hilda and Corc, though he still lacks a friend his own age."

"Sounds like you'll have some privacy on occasion, Braden." Roddy waggled his brow at his cousin. "Send Steenie to your parents, then to Hilda and Corc."

Braden chuckled. "I think we may take advantage of that."

Roddy added, "Maggie said to tell you that they found the parents of the other three lassies. She said 'twas quite touching to watch the reunions. They'd been stolen in the middle of the night."

"Bastards. By the Lamonts?" Braden asked.

"They actually never saw the thieves so they have no idea."

A comfortable silence settled between them as they considered all that had transpired. Braden said, "I know not how you two feel, but 'tis a blight we must fix if we can."

Loki said, "And we will, but now I'm hoping you'll tell me that I can eat while I'm helping you get this place in shape. How are the kitchens?"

"Aye, Cairstine's sire built one of the biggest hearths for cooking I've ever seen. The kitchens need cleaning like any other area of the keep, but with a good scrubbing, they'll be operating. Hilda and Corc have been working in there. Hilda said she would cook, but I'd be glad to have another to help her. She's promised us a rabbit stew for this eve."

Roddy said, "You've got your own castle, cousin." He slapped him on the back with a grin.

Braden nodded, pleased with how everything had unfolded. "I need more here to join us. Think on it when you return, Roddy. Talk to Uncle Alex, but I'll travel back to speak with Ronan's family. Moray could stay back as protection, and his mother could be a help to Hilda." Things were coming together, just as he and Cairstine had dreamed. One day their keep would be vibrant and full. "Aye, if Moray moves here, I'll definitely go with you. In fact, I have an idea about who might have taken up the trade. I'd like to find him before he comes after me."

"Who?" Loki asked.

"Blair Lamont. No one has seen or heard from him. He could have resurfaced, but if he has, he should be easy to track. He's not the smartest."

"It could be any number of fools out there," Roddy said. "But let's find them before they steal any more bairns."

Braden nodded. "I'm happy to join you."

Roddy had an expression on his face Braden had seen before, and it only meant one thing.

Nothing would stop him. Roddy was on the hunt.

Cairstine came out to join them, walking into Braden's arms as he kissed her cheek. He told her what they'd discussed. "We'd bring two more to join us. I'd feel better having a few more guards here with us. Mayhap we can convince a couple more to come along with Moray."

She nodded. "I'd feel better, too. It's a great idea, but…"

"What?"

"I feel as though something is missing. I can't say what, but something…" Her voice stopped midsentence because they were interrupted.

A ruckus out by the gates stunted their conversation. The portcullis had been dropped after Loki came in apparently. Something banged again and again, but it was too loud to be a knock from a person.

"What in hellfire could that be?" Braden asked, glancing at Loki and Roddy. "Did you see aught unusual when you arrived?"

Loki shook his head, then glanced at Roddy who also shook his head. "Not that I saw. Mayhap a boar?"

"Too loud for a boar." Braden hurried over to the guards' tower in the corner, climbing the stairs two at a time to look over the curtain wall to see what was causing the commotion. He glanced over the front of the wall toward the entrance, shocked at what he saw.

Loki shouted, "What the hell is it? 'Tis not stopping at all."

Roddy climbed the stairs to look over the wall with his cousin. He yelled back at Loki, "Shite, you wouldn't believe it if we told you."

"What is it?"

Roddy said, "A horse kicking the gate with its hind legs."

Braden said, "Nay, not a horse. 'Tis a pony."

Loki chuckled. "Open the gate. I can handle a wee Highland pony. I wish to see what the hell the beast could want."

Braden lifted the portcullis then raced back down the stairs and joined Cairstine to watch the pony together. Once the gates were lifted, the pony turned around and strolled through the gates as if he belonged inside.

Roddy's eyes widened. "I've never seen aught like it. What do you suppose he wants?"

They stood back to see where the pony would go. He marched between the three of them, paused long enough to shake his head and lift it with a nicker, then moved past them.

Loki drawled, "I think he just thanked us, Braden."

Braden couldn't believe his eyes. He'd never seen an animal like it. The pony headed straight for the keep. "Loki, grab the reins and stop him. He's headed for the keep with all the bairns."

Loki went after him, but the animal turned around, bared its teeth at him, then lifted its hind legs as a warning. Then he snorted, turned around, and continued his trek toward the keep.

"What could he want?" Cairstine asked, keeping a safe distance from the wee beast.

Roddy looked at Loki who shrugged his shoulders. "I don't know what he wants."

Braden said, "Let him go. We'll see what he's after. He can't break the door down. We don't have a barrel full of apples there. What could he possibly be looking for?"

The pony lifted his head, nodded twice, and crossed the courtyard, click-clacking across the stones with purpose and pride.

The door flew open and Steenie charged out the door, raced across the courtyard, threw himself at the pony and cried, "Paddy!"

Braden stood there aghast, his hands on his hips. "Steenie? You know this pony?"

"Aye, 'tis my special pet, Paddy the Pony. He found me in the middle of the night when I was lost. He brought me to Grant land. Do you not remember? Do you not love him, Mama?"

The pony leaned his head down to nuzzle Steenie who broke into a fit of giggles and threw his arms around the beast's neck. "I love you, too, Paddy."

Loki said, "I thought he looked familiar. I should have recognized him. He has a mind of his own, that one."

His sire had followed Steenie out the door. Brodie Grant looked at his son and said, "Don't question it, Braden. Take my advice and accept it as part of the unknown that you just have to trust." Then he pointed to his other son, Loki, and said, "I did the same thing with him many years ago."

Loki got a huge grin on his face. "The Highlands are indeed a magical place. 'Tis the mountains."

"So can we keep Paddy, Grandpapa?"

His sire glanced at him, quirking his brow, clearly passing the question over to him.

The animal took its time and looked at each man individually. Cairstine moved over to pet his neck, gingerly at first, but the animal allowed it. "Steenie, he's a beautiful animal. Where did you find him?"

"I got lost one night and he found me. I told you. He brought me to Uncle Loki and Kenzie, and they brought me to Clan Grant. Can I keep him? Please?"

Roddy leaned toward Loki and whispered, "I'm not telling him nay."

"Not me," Loki said. "I love ponies."

Braden couldn't help but feel there was something quite special about Paddy the Pony. He'd been a friend to a wee lad when he'd needed it most. He glanced at his sire who stood there watching him with a grin on his face.

"Braden," Cairstine said. "This is what we've been missing." She reached out to run her fingers through the animal's light-colored mane.

"Thank you, my wee friend," she whispered as she rubbed her hand down his fur. "Paddy's a bit of Highland magic, all by himself." She spun around to look at her husband. "He's just what we need. A pet for Steenie."

Braden moved closer and reached to pat Paddy's head, but the small horse snorted and shook his head before glaring at him. He took a step back and said, "Steenie, I don't see why not. We have plenty of room in the stables for your new pet."

"Yay!" shouted Steenie as the two headed toward the stables.

His sire, Loki, and Roddy all chuckled before they headed toward the keep.

Braden wrapped his arm around Cairstine and she leaned her head on his shoulder, her gaze following her son and his new pet.

"Paddy and Steenie are perfect for each other."

Braden looked into her eyes that were as green as the sprawling hills of the Highlands and saw his future in them. "Just as we are," he said.

THE END

DEAR READERS,

Thank you for reading *Highland Retribution*! I hope you enjoyed reading about Braden, Cairstine, Steenie, and Paddy the Pony. You never know when a wee bit of magic will show up in my novels.

I have several more novels planned for The Band of Cousins, but I'm going to take a break to work on the novel in the trilogy I'm writing in a collaboration with Cecelia Mecca and Emma Prince. I'm so excited about this novel because it's a time-travel story, something new for me, but I promise there will still be some strapping Highlanders for you to enjoy.

The next novel in this series will be Roddy's story.

Happy reading, and I so appreciate you following me on this journey.

As always, reviews would be greatly appreciated. Sign up for my newsletter on my website at *www.keiramontclair.com*. I send newsletters out with each new release.

Another way to receive notices about my new releases is to follow me on BookBub. Click on the tab in the upper right-hand side of my profile page. You can also write a review on BookBub.

Keira Montclair

www.keiramontclair.com
www.facebook.com/KeiraMontclair
www.pinterest.com/KeiraMontclair

NOVELS BY KEIRA MONTCLAIR

THE BAND OF COUSINS
HIGHLAND VENGEANCE
HIGHLAND ABDUCTION
HIGHLAND RETRIBUTION

THE CLAN GRANT SERIES
#1- RESCUED BY A HIGHLANDER-
Alex and Maddie
#2- HEALING A HIGHLANDER'S HEART-
Brenna and Quade
#3- LOVE LETTERS FROM LARGS-
Brodie and Celestina
#4-JOURNEY TO THE HIGHLANDS-
Robbie and Caralyn
#5-HIGHLAND SPARKS-
Logan and Gwyneth
#6-MY DESPERATE HIGHLANDER-
Micheil and Diana
#7-THE BRIGHTEST STAR IN THE
HIGHLANDS-Jennie and Aedan
#8- HIGHLAND HARMONY-
Avelina and Drew

THE HIGHLAND CLAN
LOKI-Book One
TORRIAN-Book Two
LILY-Book Three

JAKE-Book Four
ASHLYN-Book Five
MOLLY-Book Six
JAMIE AND GRACIE- Book Seven
SORCHA-Book Eight
KYLA-Book Nine
BETHIA-Book Ten
LOKI'S CHRISTMAS STORY-Book Eleven

THE SOULMATE CHRONICLES
#1 TRUSTING A HIGHLANDER

THE SUMMERHILL SERIES-
CONTEMPORARY ROMANCE
#1-ONE SUMMERHILL DAY
#2-A FRESH START FOR TWO
#3-THREE REASONS TO LOVE

REGENCY
THE DUKE AND THE DRESSMAKER

ABOUT THE AUTHOR

KEIRA MONTCLAIR IS THE PEN name of an author who lives in Florida with her husband. She loves to write fast-paced, emotional romance, especially with children as secondary characters in her stories.

She has worked as a registered nurse in pediatrics and recovery room nursing. Teaching is another of her loves, and she has taught both high school mathematics and practical nursing.

Now she loves to spend her time writing, but there isn't enough time to write everything she wants! Her Highlander Clan Grant series, comprising of eight standalone novels, is a reader favorite. Her third series, The Highland Clan, set twenty years after the Clan Grant series, focuses on the Grant/Ramsay descendants. She also has a contemporary series set in The Finger Lakes of Western New York and a paranormal historical series, The Soulmate Chronicles.

Her latest series, The Band of Cousins, stems from The Highland Clan but is a stand-alone series.

Contact her through her website, *www.keiramontclair.com*.